Bullet Tooth

Grant Wamack

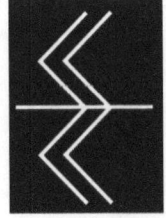

Broken River Books

MERCURIAL

CUT

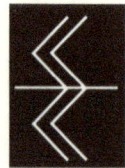

A Broken River Books Original
BROKEN RIVER BOOKS
Oklahoma City, OK
Copyright © 2024 by Grant Wamack
Cover art by Chris Fryant
IG @chrisfryant
Interior layout design by Kelby Losack
www.kelbylosack.com

ISBN: 978-1-940885-64-3

Printed in the U.S.A.

ADVANCE PRAISE FOR BULLET TOOTH

"With *Bullet Tooth*, Grant Wamack has created a horror icon for our time. Unlike Freddy and Jason who commit their violent acts with their own two hands, the titular antagonist gorges himself on the violence he encourages in people just like us. The classical sensibilities that made those previous texts work are fully intact here too, but Grant brilliantly reinterprets them for our new dark age in a voice uniquely his. If you like cursed media, iconic horror villains, or urban legends, this book is an absolute must-read."
—Lucas Mangum, author of *Gods of the Dark Web* and *Bladejob*

"Hip, fresh, with buckets of imagination and no punches pulled. I guarantee you've never read anything quite like this one, it's as deadly and unexpected as a bullet!" —Paul Kane, award-winning #1 bestselling author of *Sherlock Holmes and the Servants of Hell*, *Before*, and *The Storm*

"Grant Wamack's clean and fluid prose allows for complete immersion in the neatly interwoven stories of his compelling characters and their eventual coming together to overcome the evil unleashed from a dumpster VHS tape. Bullet Tooth as a villain is right fucked in the best way, while the lives of those who are fated to battle him have all provided unique skill sets that coalesce toward a satisfying conclusion. Hilarious, sincere, and grotesque, Wamack isn't fucking around." —Charlene Elsby, author of *The Devil Thinks I'm Pretty* and *Violent Faculties*

"Money, murder, mayhem; *Bullet Tooth* is *Sinister* if Bagul wasn't afraid to go to Chicago and he preyed on gang members instead of children. Wamack's prose is immersive in its authenticity, bringing the streets of the 'Raq to the pages of this book. Vengeance and violence, gangs and guns, load up your extendos and hundred-round drums and join me in songs of praise for *Bullet Tooth*." —David Simmons, author of *Ghosts of East Baltimore*

Dedicated to Teresa Pollack

"A city that was to forge out of steel and blood-red neon its own peculiar wilderness." - Nelson Algren.

PART ONE

BULLETS HAVE NO NAMES

Wet Renaissance

It floated inside the heart of a murky yellow void, the consistency of mucus and egg yolk.

Genderless.

Halfway sleeping, halfway awake.

Dreaming of war, dreaming of machine guns rattling into the night, dreaming of a medley of magazines shoved into mag wells, relishing the rancid scent of death while a small green vein twitched on the bulbous plain of its oversized forehead. A potpourri of bullets hovered around its deformed upper body while a blue tongue protruded from the entity's skewed mouth in a thick spiraling curl of saliva.

Volcanic rocks drifted in and out of the space. Spent cartridges, hollow points, trounds, cannonballs, wad cutters, round stones, scorched magazines, shotgun slugs, artillery shells, grenades, lead balls, and projectiles dotted the space like a mosaic of violent stars.

The space in question was relatively unknown to humans, somewhere just out of reach of hallucinogens breaking the fourth wall of human consciousness. The entity reigning over the space was once notated in the Library of Alexandria, a single grimoire buried 12 ft deep under the nation's capital, and depicted in a series Hermetic texts and occult pamphlets. It existed in another space entirely, a liminal realm of desperation, a prolific cloud of violence and ill-intent. Rotating in a woozy motion, *it* felt a slight disturbance ripple outward, a familiar rumble ran through its knotted musculature, a soft cluster of vibrations, a series of ancient intonations resonating throughout its atomic makeup.

Someone was calling.

Someone was calling its name.

No, *his* name. Cells flowed together like grains of sand, spongy tissue and blood vessels formed into a perfect scrotum. Genitalia bloomed in between his lean legs padded with muscle, and testosterone flowed into his bloodstream at a rapid pace.

Bullet-tooooothhhhhhh.

Bullet-tooooothhhhhhh.

Bullet-tooooothhhhhhh.

It was the most comforting song. A swaying lullaby of death with technological clicks in the distance. A hyperviolent summoning.

Bullet-tooooothhhhhhh.

Eyes the color of sangria snapped open, and Bullet Tooth took a deep breath into ancient lungs. One smooth exhale and tectonic plates slipped on the New Madrid Fault Line, triggering a magnitude 5 earthquake throughout the Midwest.

Illinois somehow experienced the worst impact, receiving the full brunt of the natural disaster, one of 12 states sustaining substantial damage within the region. Fifteen people killed and 37 injured. Seismologists claimed this occurrence only happened every 20 years, a freak accident, fresh fodder for the hungry news outlets and social media platforms, churning out fear-ridden stories and heavy-handed documentation of the aftermath.

Satisfactory, Bullet Tooth thought to himself, assessing the full extent of the chaos and ruin he caused through remote viewing. He grinned, exposing a set of gold incendiary bullets bursting out of his pink puffy gums. Some were rusted and coated in grime while others shimmered under the rays of an invisible light.

"I'm coming, my child," he snorted a thick cloud of fear and violence originating in the Midwest through a thin seam in the dimensional makeup of Earth, slowly gaining strength and vigor.

"Don't you worry, I hear your call."

A Fated Meeting

Caleb rapidly slid his thumb upwards, scrolling through pictures of abstract art. A digital galleria of raw messy strokes covered the paintings he stared at, trying his best to decipher the underlying emotions, soaking up the visceral sense of expression and messy emotions dripping from the edges of his phone's cracked screen.

The doorbell jingled as someone new shuffled inside the barbershop's entrance. Caleb looked up, noticing the neighborhood's bootleg man taking his ragged backpack off his hunched shoulders and rummaging around inside for a fresh stack of DVDs. He wore a thick navy-blue bubble vest, and a black stocking cap with the words "Chicago Over Everything" covering his short hair. His goatee was overgrown and patchy with a few grays present. Reeked of garlic and cigarettes. His dry lips moved a million miles per minute, spilling out a well-practiced sales pitch despite his slow advance. It was a sight to behold.

"D-V-Ds, get your D-V-Ds! I have the hottest movies out for the most affordable prices."

Trying his best not to be seen or noticed, Caleb tossed his black hood over his blond dyed dreads and pulled the drawstrings downward with force, nearly eclipsing his line of sight and muffling the sounds within a 10 ft. radius of his chair. He visualized himself blending in with his surroundings, melting into the white walls behind him like a melanated chameleon.

Be one with the walls. Be one with the walls. Be one—

"Young man, I forget your name, but I haven't forgotten your face...Would you be interested in some bootlegs? We got some new ones in. That good shit by the way."

The bootleg man displayed a small stack of DVDs with cheaply photoshopped movie covers, waving them around like lottery tickets. They might as well have been relics from another time to Caleb.

I wouldn't take that shit for free, he thought, hoping his true feelings wouldn't surface on his face.

"I got *La La Land, Terrifier, The Void, Suicide Squad, Mandy, Knives Out.* Matter of fact, I got a whole deal going just for you. Student discount and a three for one special. No better deal in the Windy City. How about that?"

"No thanks."

"Come on, this is literally a steal and I know you like movies. These are cinematic experiences. I used to run to the movie theater when I was your age..." The bootleg man trailed off, lost inside a mental bog of glitched-out memories and whiskey-laced nostalgia.

Caleb looked to his barber Malik who gave him a sly grin and a shrug before returning to cutting his client's thick head of hair.

"Let me ask you something, no disrespect or anything, but have you heard of streaming?" Caleb asked.

"Yeah, it's killing my hustle. *Streaming,*" The bootleg man said the last word with the utmost disgust and resentment. "I'm one of the last of my kind doing what I do. A dying breed in fact. Forcing me to develop passive streams of income."

"What type of streams?" Caleb asked, genuinely curious.

"That's a work in progress... anyway, I'm telling you, nothing beats physical media. The sheer quality is unparalleled."

"Alright, how about this? I'll buy something next time I see you. I promise." Caleb immediately wished he could have gone back in time and yanked his vocal cords out of his throat like a bundle of electric cords, but it was far too late and he wanted to end this conversation. He was a man of his word and he'd have to follow through the next time he saw the bootleg man.

"Next time. What if there isn't a next time?" The bootleg man moved into Caleb's personal bubble with no regard for the teenager's boundaries. His eyes were bulging, red veins forming a distinctive map of arteries embedded in the geography of his sclera.

Caleb sunk deeper into his stiff chair, neck muscles growing tense. He thought about punching the nigga in the face, but didn't want to catch an assault charge. That's the last thing he needed today.

"Niggas get shot everyday," the bootleg man squeezed Caleb's shoulder. "Check the statistics. Read the *Chicago Tribune* or the *Sun-Times*. It don't matter if you're a rapper, a working man or a student with a fresh face like yours. Everyone's a target out here and I'm no exception."

Caleb's heartbeat sped up, the muscular organ lodged inside his chest felt like a 40lb. kettlebell, anxiety spreading through his throat like a slow-moving infection, the buzz of electric clippers applying pressure to the base of his eardrums, the thick clumps of black hair on the floor twitching like dead rats, tears beginning to form in the tender ducts of his closed eyes.

Don't let these niggas see you cry, he told himself, knowing any sign of weakness would follow you like a ghost throughout the city, marking you as potential prey.

Malik had seen enough and jumped in. "Leave that nigga alone and stop speaking that negativity in here. You know words have power. Don't manifest that shit, goddamnit."

"I'm just speaking my truth, nigga," the bootleg man huffed. "My ancestors fought for the freedom of speech and I'm going to speak it. It's my American right."

"Go tell it to the Mayor then, nigga," Malik said.

The bootleg man stuffed the DVDs back into his bag and looked around the shop for anyone showing signs of interest. Everyone avoided eye contact, so he sauntered back over to Caleb.

Caleb braced himself for whatever was about to happen next.

"I'm sorry if I scared ya. Sometimes I lose sight of my social graces. Still hit me up if you need some fresh movies in your life."

"It's all good."

The bootleg man shuffled back outside the store, fussing on his way out with zero sales and a heavy heart.

Caleb took a series of deep breaths, waiting for his heart rate to slow down and his anxiety to dissipate. He checked his pockets for pills, but there was only lint.

Malik cleared his throat. "You okay?"

Caleb wanted to be honest and say no, he wanted to speak up and tell the whole goddamn shop he was on the edge of a breakdown and the mercurial nature of his emotions were getting the best of him, but he shoved those thoughts aside and said, "Yeah."

"You still seeing that therapist?" Malik handed his client a mirror.

"Yeah a couple times a month. It helps, I guess."

"I just want to make sure you're doing okay especially after—"

"—I know. You don't have to say it." The tears almost came back. Caleb pushed them away, commanding his body to become emotionless again.

A numb vessel.

"I'm sorry, man," Malik looked visibly concerned. "I just want you to know I worry. You're like a second son to me. And you know your pops made me promise to look after you."

"It's all good. And I appreciate it. I'm just not up for talking about it right now, but I'm okay. I really am."

We both know I'm lying my ass off. Hopefully, he buys it.

"You sure?" Malik asked, most likely seeing through the veneer.

Caleb looked Malik in the eyes and feigned his best smile possible.

"Yeah, I'm great."

Analog Lines

The bootleg man shuffled down the alleyway, following a hunch inside his gut, a dim feeling of fortune present in the air. His real name was Devin Greene, but he liked being known as the local bootleg man. The moniker filled him with a warm sense of pride, gave him a mythical air, and a dream-like proximity akin to the gawds above and below.

Earlier in the day, he snuck into the back door of a local theater on its last leg. It had seen much better days, but thanks to multiple economic downturns, streaming services, and inflation, the theater was in severe debt and the acne-prone teenage workers didn't care if an old man with a camera weaseled his way inside. The velvet carpet had large holes, questionable stains, and a strange odor, but it brought the bootleg man great comfort. This was something tangible he could step foot on, something with age that he could appreciate like himself. It had character.

Filming was easy and the bulky camera mounted on his shoulder was like an old friend. He filmed every movie that came out at showtimes that were sparse and unrealistic for families. Something about the primordial darkness and solitude felt like a warm womb, like he was returning back to some maternal beginning inside the deserted theater.

These pleasant memories drifted away as he stepped over a gaping pothole with a condom floating in the center like a bone-yellow oculus. A shiver ran down his spine as he continued moving down the alley, digging his finger into his right ear. Stimulating the acupressure point calmed his nerves.

A few cardboard boxes sat outside a massive green dumpster. A layer of snow covered the green lid. It smelled like spoiled eggs and toilet water even with the cold weather. Despite the smell, the bootleg man could sense treasure amidst the heaps of trash, waiting to be discovered.

"What do we have here?" He said as he moved closer, excitement running through every step.

His knees ached as he hunched forward to see what was inside the first box. Dipping his brown hands into the darkness, he pulled out a rabbit shaped kiddie bank with cracks running through the belly and a few oversized sweaters littered with gaping holes. He looked inside the second box and gasped.

My lucky day.

He couldn't believe it. The box was full of VHS tapes. They were unmarked, dried mud clumped on the outside of a few, but they seemed to be in good working condition. One tape had a filthy sticker running along the side that said PROJECT BULLET BABY. He never heard of that movie and he considered himself a diehard cinephile, but he figured he could always clean these up and make them like new.

I've never been afraid of some hard work and mom used to say I have a good eye for detail. Might be able to fetch a pretty penny for these. You never know what could be on here.

His knees popped loudly as he stood, pouring the videos into his bag. He grinned, hefting the weight of his new possessions over his shoulder. He thought about selling them to older folk who had an appreciation for these films. Then he considered running home and checking out the videos himself, but something in his gut gave him a firm no.

Don't sniff your own supply, his OG once told him when he was much younger. Mind you, he didn't sell drugs, but he still hustled product even if it was purely analog.

And the almighty dollar was calling his name like a siren in the night.

Hennything's Possible

The custom Glock gleamed underneath the red light of the silicone strawberry lamp, the outline of a white tiger head emblazoned on the muzzle like an animalistic familiar, cherry red eyes blazing like two twin suns against the darkness of the black gunmetal.

Jasmine Nasrallah sat cross-legged with her phone propped up on a pink shoebox, cleaning her new gun. The phone's camera captured her strong cheekbones, oval face, and large yet mesmerizing brown eyes as she sat on her bed during a live video.

A few years ago, someone claiming to be a distant cousin had mailed her a bundle of handwritten letters from her mom who passed when she was three in Palestine. Her mom said she had been blessed by the daughters of Allah with a rare beauty, the compliments bringing her to tears every single time she read them. She briefly thought about those letters as she stared into the eye of the phone's camera and admired herself.

Jasmine's father Jamal Crawford served in the Air Force as an enlisted airman, rumors about his time working unique jobs as special forces reconnaissance, but it was hush hush. Despite pressing her cousins for more information, they wouldn't spill another word. He met her mom, they fell in love and conceived Jasmine under an azure sky. That was years before the unmarked warplanes flew overhead, carpet bombing her parents' home.

Comments and hearts flooded the screen and donations slowly trickled into her digital tip jar. Random usernames tried shooting their shot, hoping their words could digitally seduce her, but she didn't pay them any mind. She was floating in her own world, enthralled by the distinct *cha-ching* emanating from the phone's speaker over and over again.

Drill rap music poured out of the hot pink Kawaii from the speaker planted on her desk, bunny ears poking out the base like antennas. King Von was rapping frantically, barely taking a breath, relaying a compelling tale about gunning down opps and smoking on Tooka packs on the Southside of Chicago.

"I'll push yo shit back."

Jasmine rapped along empathically, wiping the barrel of her Glock down with a newfound vigor in synch with the beat. She took great care of her gun collection, keeping them clean and in great working order. She imagined her parents would be proud of her if she ever got a chance to know them. She was an orphan, raised by the state of Illinois. She wasn't what you would call foster home material, but she managed to get her own place and make something of herself. The American dream...

"If you know, you know, nigga," she said, grinning.

tWilightx99 commented — *luv you lots. You're so pretty.*

PushinPGeneralll commented — *love your cleavage* *eggplant emoji* *show us your tits.*

MentallyIllestX commented — *you're pretty for a sand nigga.*

RicardobORNedEAD5 commented — *I would cut off my left hand and sell my balls on the black market just so you can hold me the way you hold that gun* *demon emoji and water splash emoji*

Meangurl203 commented — *What's your favorite color?*

LikeGrah777 commented — *Spit on me mommy and step on my throat.*

TraumatizedBoi commented — *Gun waifu, please me make me your paypig and take my life savings as tribute.*

Jasmine cringed. "C'mon guys, no perverts allowed on my lives. That shit will get you blocked. I'm not playing around. Can I get a real question of substance before I shut this down? I'm trying to be nice, and you aren't making it easy."

Twiglet212 commented — *how do you stay so confident? What's your secret? Please spill sis...*

"Alright, babes," she said in an exaggerated voice—feminine with the soft hint of a childish tone. "From one bitch to another, you have to fake it til you make it. I used to be sad and depressed, thinking about the parents I never had, my people suffering in Palestine, and even stressed about my body. Wished I had bigger boobs," she squeezed her A-cup breasts. "I mean God did grace me with an ass and a pretty face, but I can thank my genes for that. For years, I struggled to find my identity especially being half black and half Palestinian, but I had to learn how to accept me for me. It took a lot of inner work, positive self-talk, therapy, and affirmations to get here. Plus, lots of water and skin care."

Twiglet222 commented — *thank you* *big dramatic heart emojis flooded the screen before fading into the digital ether.*

"You're welcome, babe. Self-love is the best love. That's the foundation and garden in which everything grows from."

Jasmine cocked her Glock, smiling.

She sang along to a few auto-tuned songs before blowing a kiss into the screen and ending the live video with her signature saying. "And remember babes, Hennything's possible."

Checking the number of donations made her eyes light up and she was beaming. She did the math in her head, calculating rough estimates and numbers.

Might be able to cop that Draco soon and flex on these niggas. I could take out the entire patriarchy myself if I have to.

She thought about the Draco AK-47 with the chrome-lined barrel. Swimming into the deep end of a well-cultivated fantasy, she pictured herself taking photos with it, the camera flash highlighting her flawless skin, feeling the full weight of the weapon in her hands, the sheer power buzzing through her frame. It would be hers in just a matter of weeks. Shit, maybe even sooner.

She put her Glock away in a silver case, treating it like a baby with the utmost care, consideration, and compassion. Locked the case shut and shoved it under her desk. Turning out the lights, she slipped into bed, hoping to take a nap.

From her phone, she donated a few thousand dollars to the Palestine Children's Relief Fund, feeling like she was correcting some vital wrong in the world, potentially opening a door for some young brown girl like her in need of a helping hand.

Growing restless, Jasmine turned her light back on and moved a strand of black hair behind her ear. She switched on her Dremel DigiLab 3D printer, automatically connecting to her pink iPad, with a Berserk sigil sticker on the back, and a smattering of pink gun stickers, one saying Pew Pew Pew, surrounded by small mauve roses.

"Time to get to work, Digi." She rubbed the 3D printer, hoping her soft words of encouragement would help it produce the best pieces possible. She bought it on whim, but after successfully printing and putting together auto sears, more commonly known as switches, for her own guns, she realized the immense potential lying dormant within the machine. This small device could be easily installed on the back of a handgun and give weapons the capability of firing until the trigger was lifted.

Niggas needed to expand their weaponry and she was ready to fulfill the demand. She got in good with some Gangster Disciples, Black Disciples, and had been trying to link up with a Vice Lord, but she couldn't find a reliable link with the gang. She knew if she stayed persistent, she'd find a way with time.

She printed out five switches, fulfilling her quota for today's orders. The auto sears resembled Lego pieces that could turn an ordinary citizen into a force of nature. Customers would hit her up on the Signal app, messages encrypted and untraceable. If she ever got a bad feeling about someone, she'd wipe the number clean and start the process over from scratch. Customers always found her, and word of mouth spread through the proper channels like wildfire.

Jasmine carefully wrapped the switches in happy birthday wrapping paper and placed them in celebratory bags with cute handles. No one would question an unassuming petite girl with gifts in hand. She planned to make the drop off at a Chevron gas station. Safe territory for her since she was cool with the clerks and she was packing heat at all times.

Her phone dinged with a fresh notification, and she checked her direct messages from a muscle-bound man with a strange tattoo covering his bald head who claimed to be Vice Lord. He had a weird aura about him that made her nervous yet drew her into the eye of the storm.

"Heard you know how to wrap gifts? I would love to procure your services pretty lady."

She smiled at the compliment, but forced herself to stay in business mode. Scrolled through his photos, feeling him out. She could tell he had money and something about him screamed danger, but she was going to say yes from the moment she laid eyes on him.

Feeling a bit devilish, Jasmine decided she would make him wait a bit before responding. She never wanted customers to look at her like an easy target, especially since she was a woman. Jasmine was the furthest thing from thirsty so she would make him wait.

In the meantime, she had to get ready for the drop-off. She put away the product, turned the light back out, and slipped back into bed, growing sleepy. She clicked on her essential oil diffuser, which helped ease her deeper into sleep once she got comfortable in bed.

Closing her almond brown eyes, she fantasized about niggas kicking in her door and her unphased, grabbing the Draco from underneath the bed. Brandishing the Romanian pistol proudly, pulling the trigger, and letting the banana clip sing.

Livers exploding, kidneys punctured, blood splatter painting the walls in an explosive fashion. Sweet flowery notes of ylang ylang punctuated the violence.

Her fingers traveled down south, crawling past the waistband of her thong, snaking into the lips of her vagina, seeking the wetness growing inside of her. *Pleasure is the ultimate form of liberation.*

She stuffed three fingers inside, masturbating. With her free hand, she found her clitoris and started rubbing it in a clockwise motion, moaning softly. She arched her back slightly, riding the waves of pleasure.

Pop. Pop. Pop. Pop.

Bodies stacked on the floor, slowly growing into a tower of flesh nearly reaching the ceiling.

Biting her bottom lip, she shoved her fingers even deeper into her vagina, increasing the pace. Her hand moved away from her clit and gripped the pillow behind her head, sweat breaking out on her forehead as she embraced the sweet release and swam into the eye of euphoria.

Left Hook from Hell

Weights clinked, jump ropes whipped through the air, leather mitts punched by weathered gloves, punk rock music blasted out of the speakers inside the grungy boxing gym, distorted drums percolated through the air, and a thick layer of sweaty condensation covered the walls like a milky film.

Fredo Vargas blinked through the sweat dripping down his eyes into his thick beard, wearing a sweat-drenched shirt clinging to his chest like a leech, a visceral Rorschach test embedded into several threads of polyester. He threw a series of furious combos on the heavy bag, channeling his anger into his 12 oz gloves. Jab, jab, jab, right cross, uppercut. He took a step back, breathing in through his nose and exhaling through his mouth. Bouncing on his toes the whole time. Regrouping for more pugilistic mayhem.

He heard the ghost of his coach's gruff voice bleed through his headphones. "Listen here and listen good, this is the last round. The fight is too close to call. You have to go in for the kill, Fredo. Fuck that nigga up."

Moving off a combination of muscle memory and killer instinct, Fredo threw a hard right hook, rotating his hips to amass the appropriate amount of force behind the punch, remembering how satisfying flesh crunching beneath his punches felt, picturing an old opponent stunned, staggering backward on the bloodied canvas. He followed it up with a quick one-two, and ended the combo with a series of sharp body shots, punctuated by a left hook from hell.

The anger flowed out of him like a massive exhaust pipe, unloading everything he had onto the bag, energetically bleeding out of his gloves, and sapping his body of emotion. Everything went blurry for a moment and anxiety swelled up in his gut, hardening into a glacier. The seasoned boxers, the swaying heavy bag, and the boxing ring moved in and out of his perception. Blobs of pixels. Fredo closed his eyes, trying to shake it off and force his brain to filter reality correctly.

Keep it together. You're alright. You're alright.

Everything came back into a dizzying focus and the anxiety slowly melted away. He was alright and he was thankful he didn't faint. Never would have heard the end of it from the other guys in the gym.

Maybe I need to listen to my ex and get my brain scanned.

Fredo pushed the paranoia down in his mind to a place where he wouldn't worry about brain damage, CTE, or encephalopathy potentially budding inside the soft tissue underneath his skull. He tried wiping the sweat off his tatted head devoid of hair, but quickly realized it was useless with gloves covering his big hands. The intricate geometric patterns tatted across the curved plane of his bald head glistened underneath the fluorescent lights. Fat beads of sweat dripped down from his thick beard, imprinting his presence in the gym's DNA.

I'm ungrounded. Need to eat something. Need some fuel.

He sat down in a metal foldup chair, grateful for the stability, took off his gloves, and began undoing his handwraps. One hundred dollar bills printed on the gauze with Benjamin

Franklin sporting a black eye. The wraps made him feel more abundant, made him feel like he could make a ton of money if he sweated his essence into the fabric. Maybe even strengthen his ability to manifest a financial windfall out of thin air.

"Money on my mind," he lazily sang. "Money on my mind."

His phone vibrated, interrupting his listless singing.

"Who the fuck?" He looked down and saw someone was calling him from WhatsApp. Must be a client. *Business, baby.*

"Hello?"

"H-hello?"

"You called me?" Fredo said looking around the gym for an eavesdropper, but everyone was consumed in their own world, too focused on their own quest for greatness.

"I heard you sell super soakers?" Guy had a weird accent, hard to place. *Asian maybe?*

"I might be in the business of procuring super soakers..."

"For my two sons of course."

"Why not hit up a toy store? They got plenty and then some."

"I heard you have the old-school super soakers. The ones they took off the market years ago. I get nostalgic sometimes. Want my kids to experience something real. Something timeless." The guy sneezed.

Nasty fuck.

"Bless you. You sick or something? I don't want to catch a virus meeting you in person. No offense."

"No offense taken."

"Well it's your lucky day bro. I have a large assortment of super soakers that just came in last week."

"Fantastic, but I would like to meet you first before we get down to business."

"This is a transaction, not a meet and greet bro."

"I understand, but I get paranoid. I'm just getting to know you and I have no feel for your character."

"Where would you want to meet? Chicago's a big fuckin city."

"There's an underground party on the Southside..."

Fredo typed the address, date, and time into his notes app. He wondered if this was an elaborate set-up. Didn't understand why he had to attend a fucking party to secure this job, but he needed the money. Business had been slow this month and Fredo could almost smell the stink of money coming through the encrypted line.

A young nigga was about to come up. Might as well celebrate, right?

Right?

Free Smoke

Jasmine pulled up to the gun range in a big poofy pink jacket, black cargo joggers, a black beanie, and a pair of Chanel butterfly shades. After shutting off the ignition and grabbing her gun case, she stepped outside into the frigid cold. She could see her breath rise out of her mouth like a phantasm.

She paused and snapped a couple of quick selfies, collecting social media content for the day and quite possibly for the days ahead. It was a lot of work, constantly documenting nearly every moment of her life, but it helped bring in sponsorships, a rush of views, likes, shares, and the energy exerted paid in dividends.

Tom Alderton sat at the front counter with his legs kicked up as he typed away on his laptop. He sighed when he heard the front door jingle, but his disposition changed with the quickness once he set eyes on Jasmine.

"Ah Jas, how are you doing today?" He said, putting the laptop aside, sweeping his legs down and leaning forward on the desk. Hands clasped as if he was in prayer.

"I'm good, but I'm about to be great once I let these shots off."

"I feel you on that girl. Well you know the drill. Range is wide open right now. Slow day."

"Damn, that sucks."

"Doesn't suck when I get to see your beautiful face walk through this door."

"Awww, you're too sweet, Tommy." Jasmine smiled and dropped a stack of cash on the desk with a sly wink before grabbing a set of black tactical earmuffs and protective glasses. She walked through a red door and could feel her excitement rising to the surface. This was her Disneyland, this was her Wonderwall, this was her liberation.

She unclasped her gun case and pulled out her custom Glock. Raw unfiltered joy spilled out of her body as she loaded up an extended clip and snapped a black switch onto the back of the gun, transforming it into a machine gun in a matter of seconds.

"Let's fucking go, nigga," she said to her Glock. "We're about to make a movie. Viral."

Putting on her hearing protection and glasses, she steadied herself, willing her emotions to even out into a tranquil pond. She moved into a shooting stance, taking aim at the silhouette paper target in the distance, and pulled the trigger. The gun bucked, surprising Jasmine for a brief second, gold shell casings spilling out of the magazine at a rapid pace.

A chaotic pattern of bullet holes dotted the center mass of the target, wavering slightly to the right. Jasmine thought it was a decent starting point, but she wasn't fully satisfied with the results. If this was a real-world situation, someone might survive. Keyword being might.

Stop being so hard on yourself, Jas. You're a good shooter and the recoil took you by surprise.

Jasmine took a deep breath and pulled out a fresh magazine, readying her Glock for action. Carefully placing the emptied magazine next to her case, she stood back up, excited to let more shots off. She slammed in the extended magazine with the palm of her hand and grinned. Pulled the trigger. Driving a flurry of shots into the faceless head of the target, feeling an unbridled glee take over.

Sometimes she wondered if she had an unhealthy obsession with guns. Maybe she should ask her therapist about it during her next session, but everyone around her encouraged the hobby, labeling the fascination as a healthy outlet for stress.

She never actually had to use a gun on anyone, but she thought about it and the thoughts alone excited her to no end. If men could pose with guns with no issue and carry them on a regular basis, what was the problem with a woman doing the same?

A soft alarm rang in the distance, emanating from her phone's speaker. It was time to leave and head to the gas station for the drop-off. She hurriedly put away her Glock, magazines, and scooped up the shell casings.

"You know I shouldn't be letting you use those, could get us both locked up!" Tom said, gesturing to the switches she just tested out. "Lose my whole shit."

"Last time, I promise," she said.

"That's what you said last time," Tom shook his head, distracted by the way Jasmine's hips swayed with each step.

"Bye, Tommy," she said, putting extra emphasis on the last syllable and blowing a kiss with her free hand. Exiting the gun range, she had no idea Tom blushed at the small gesture.

It was already dark by the time she settled into her car and popped in the gas station's address into her GPS. She threw on G-Herbo's album *Survivor's Remorse* as she cruised down the streets, jarred by a set of interconnected potholes she ran over.

Ugh, my car deserves better than this...

Jasmine pulled up to the gas station, which was pretty empty except for one guy filling up his black Jeep. She was meeting up with a Gangster Disciple who already paid half up front for the switches. He was supposed to be pulling up in a white Tesla and paying the other half of their agreement in person.

It was a great spot. Cops avoided it, the cameras were faulty, and were only there for show, designed to ward off any wrongdoing or illegal activity. Too bad this façade achieved the opposite effect, only intensifying the presence of criminals.

In the meantime, she uploaded fresh pics to her social media, old pics from the gun range with the caption reading *Don't give him head, give him headshots* with a masked ninja emoji next to it. She lazily scrolled through the stream of fresh comments, spam, and DMs. It all blended together after a while outside of the verified accounts giving her compliments.

A car engine revved, breaking her social media reverie and announcing the arrival of her GD client. He went by the name of Nate online, she wasn't sure if that was a made-up name, a false identity or his government name. Either way, she didn't care as long as she got paid.

The white Tesla pulled up alongside her, clean as fuck except for a few bullet holes dotting the rear of the vehicle. The window hummed down, revealing Nate's charming smile, a black bandana tied around his forehead, thick dreads cascading down, bands of gold cinched around the middle of each one. There was a guy in the passenger seat, but his face was obscured by the lack of light. Still, Jasmine noticed two white band-aids in the shape of an X covered his nose like the end of a treasure map.

"What's crackin, juicy Jas?" Nate asked.

"Please don't call me juicy Jas," Jasmine blew air through her nostrils. "It's misogynistic and cringe."

The mysterious passenger laughed.

"My bad, Jas," Nate said, hands up in the air, more gold covering his fingers and wrists like royalty. "I was just breaking the ice, trying to get off a joke. Y'know?"

"It's all good. I just want to make sure we start off on the right foot."

"The good foot," Nate said, nodding.

"The good foot."

"So you got the goods, folk?" Nate said.

"Yeah, right here," she grabbed the birthday bag and handed it over.

Nate grabbed the bag, a wide smile appearing on his face as he inspected it. "Thanks for the gifts, gang. I feel touched that you remembered my birthday. I got family who can't even do that." He shook his head and feigned wiping a tear from his left eye.

"You know I can't forget about my nigga on his birthday."

Nate handed the bag over to his boy, who rummaged inside, unwrapping the gifts. "I appreciate you. You're good people."

"Thanks."

Nate pulled out a few stacks of cash, tossed it inside a black convenience store bag and handed it over.

"I threw a little extra in there for you because you're pretty and all. Consider it a tip if you catch my drift."

Jasmine wanted to throw up at the gesture, wishing men could try harder when it came to shooting their shots.

Modern-day courtship has gone to complete shit.

"Thanks," she weakly smiled.

"I think it might be time to celebrate and try these gifts out tonight. Maybe pay the opps a visit."

"Yeah, why not?" Jas said, ready to go home.

"It's my birthday, I'll cry if I want to, I'll shoot the opps if I want to," Nate lazily sang the melody. "We're smoking on a pack tonighttttt."

Jas laughed, playing along. She wondered how much longer she'd have to entertain this bullshit and feed Nate's psychotic ego.

"Alright Jas, it was real. I'm about to go celebrate in a major way." He pulled out his Glock, waving it in the air.

Nate dapped up Jasmine as he pulled off, yelling out the window...

"B-D-K. It's free smoke for these fuck niggas."

Therapy Session #1

Caleb unscrewed the lid on the brown bottle and tossed back two circular pink pills with a glass of orange juice. He bought the percs from the hypebeast plug posted outside of the corner store last week. One week his plug was wearing Supreme fitted caps and the next he had on Amiri sweats from head to toe. Either way, Caleb got lucky especially since ole boy had a sale going on, claiming the pills were on the brink of expiration. The opiates made everything softer, warmer, and quieter. Every time Caleb popped one, the dark thoughts of suicide became a soft whisper in the back of his brain, and the depressive weight he carried around became significantly lighter.

White noise.

Tossing on a bulky mustard yellow coat and lacing up his black Timbaland boots, he walked past his grandma's room, hearing the TV blare at a high volume. Gunshots, guttural screams, and a car screeching off. Probably was watching something on Tubi. She loved B-rated black movies and Caleb knew she was eating the drama up like a form of long-lost sustenance. He left the apartment without saying a word and stepped into the snow-ridden landscape.

A blue snowplow slowly cut its way through the snow, clearing half the road adjacent to Caleb's path, revealing slick asphalt. The icy wind picked up, cutting his face as he moved through the slushy sidewalk with hands shoved deep into his pockets. He pulled his zipper all the way up and tightened the drawstrings on his hood, hoping the insulation would magically heat him up. After floating through the snow for a couple of miles and taking in the sunless sky, he finally made it to the therapist's office. The sign hanging from the awning above the front entrance was askew and letters were missing. *Opmum Joy Therap*. Snow crystals dripped overhead. Grumbling, he entered the front office, thankful for the blast of heat.

"Good afternoon, I just need you to fill out this form," the woman behind the desk looked down at her cellphone, black bangs nearly covering her weary eyes, texting someone at a furious pace. Her fingers were like pale spiders moving effortlessly across the screen and she paused to hand the clipboard over.

Must have been important.

Caleb grabbed the clipboard and sat down, staring up at the flat-screen TV glitching out on the wall.

"Thousands in downtown Chicago rally for stricter gun laws. Many of the protesters..."

A news anchor's stoic face moved across the screen like beige dough, smearing into a collection of wavy lines of green and purple spiraling into vertical bars. His words became distorted gibberish, his pitch deepening, and Caleb clocked out, becoming hyper aware of his chair. He ran his hands over the blue velvet, enjoying the soft texture. So soft...almost silky in a sense. Or was his body becoming one with the chair?

He filled out the paperwork even though they had his information in the system already. *Who came up with these mindless procedures just to eat away at my time?* Returning the clipboard to the woman behind the desk, he sat back down waiting.

Staring at the ceiling, he began counting the pockmarks in the paint, desperately scrying for a pattern to emerge from the white expanse. Staring, staring, scrying, scrying, scrying. Something furry began to emerge from the drop ceiling, an opaque fungus writhing in the cracks...

"Caleb?"

He blinked rapidly and shook his head to recalibrate. Reset. Looking back up at the ceiling, it returned to normal. He stood too quickly and almost forgot how to breathe.

"You okay?" His therapist asked, her voice soothing and concerned. She was an Indian woman with a broad nose, designer glasses, defined dimples, and a calming presence. Her hair was pulled back into a strict ponytail. And she wore a thick cream-colored sweater, yellow pants, and Chelsea boots.

Calming down, Caleb nodded and followed his therapist into a cramped room with the heater grumbling and groaning in the background. Ordinarily, the heat would have been too much, but the percs thrumming through his system gave everything a pillowy dream-like edge.

This is gonna be a breeze.

"So how have you been Caleb? Since the... event?"

"Bad."

"Can you define bad please?"

"Depressed. Sad. Tired. Nihilistic... Some days I don't want to leave my bed, let alone the house."

His therapist nodded, taking down diligent notes. Her pen scratched across the paper, dictating strange characters. Caleb tried reading her poker face, searching for an emotional hint of where she was going. Licking his dry lips, he watched her white pen glide across the page and checked his pockets for his chapstick, which was missing. He could watch her write all day, eyes following the sleek curves and sharp punctuation.

"And your art, have you been drawing or painting lately?"

Caleb shrugged. "You know, here and there, but not as productive as I would like to be. Feel blocked, the anxiety gets in the way. Like there's a massive buildup of art somewhere inside of me. I just can't reach it."

"Why do you think you feel this way?"

"I don't know how to explain it... my emotions feel like this separate *thing*. It's hard to keep them together. This chaotic mass laces into everything and comes spilling out at the worst time possible. I'm so tired of crying."

"Hmmm...," she took down more notes on the legal pad, filling up the page like a psychological piece of art. Caleb wondered if she was a virtuoso in another life.

"Do you feel like expanding on that? Your emotions. Maybe you're ready to talk about *it*?"

"Yeah," Caleb rubbed his hands over the contours of his face to make sure his body was still intact. He cracked his neck. *All my joints are still here and working properly.*

"Sure."

"Well, go ahead. This is a safe space. No judgements, no diagnoses. I promise. I'm just a big ear listening." She smiled. "And you can take that hood off. The heat's on and I don't want you getting sick. Your grandma would murder me and I have a lot of living left to do."

Caleb faked a hearty laugh, took a deep breath, and pulled his hood back, unveiling his blond dreads. They *felt* luminous.

"I mean, it's been hard. Parks was like a brother to me. We came up together. Bled together. We had a *bond*. He'd seen my wins and my losses. Sports, school, girls, etc. I just can't believe those niggas shot him all because of a gang affiliation. G-D. He never hurt no body. I mean he wasn't someone to play with but still, he was good people. Didn't deserve that. Not at all."

"You're right, Caleb. He certainly didn't deserve that. No one does, but the streets can be unforgiving... Please continue. I feel like you have more to get off your chest."

Caleb cringed at her response and the ghost of anger burned inside his gut. *What the fuck did she know about the streets?*

"Ever since he was gunned down, I've been feeling lost. I wasn't codependent or anything like that, but it felt like a chunk of me had been cut out. A vital organ stolen and sold on the black market for profit. You get what I'm saying?"

"I do Caleb. I truly do. Please, go on."

"I mean what the fuck is G-D-K? How do you make a gang based off killing a specific group of people?" Tears welled up Caleb's brown eyes and he sniffled. "Larry Hoover didn't start GD's for violence and greed. He did it to cultivate a sense of community. To bring people together... not this shit."

"You're referring to Gangster Disciple Killer? Am I correct?"

"Yes, it's goofy shit. His killer is still out there screaming G-D-K. Like that is something to be proud of or something." Caleb restrained himself from spitting out the nasty taste in his mouth. "I can't believe the cops didn't catch him. No fingerprints, no DNA, nothing. It's almost as if they didn't give a fuck. Like we mean nothing to them."

"It's terrible. The police system is flawed, that's for sure. How have you been processing all of this?"

"Not much at all. I've been escaping through my art...and other things. It's cathartic in a sense."

"It's healthy to process your feelings using an outlet such as art, but you want to make sure you're properly grieving so it doesn't build up," her tone softened a few notches. "Remember, it's okay to cry. It's a ritual of sorts. A purging. You want to make sure you're releasing these emotions so you can move forward."

"You have no idea...I've cried so much," he struggled to swallow his emotions. "I just miss my friend and I want things to go back to the way they used to be. When will this shit ever end?" Hot tears streamed down Caleb's face and his therapist handed him a box of tissues. "Sorry for putting this on you."

"You don't have to apologize for your emotions. What you're feeling is important and valid, but unfortunately, we are at time," she glanced at her gold face Fendi watch with a pink leather band wrapped around her bony wrist. "I have some homework for you."

"What?"

"I want you to bring in some art next time. It's a good way to look at your emotions from an alternative angle. And *please* try to keep your head up and stay positive. Things tend to work themselves out for the better with time and compassion."

"Will they?" Caleb wiped the tears out of his eyes and threw his hood back over his head, obscuring his vision.

"They will," she nodded. "Have a good one Caleb."

He exited the office in a hurry, playing around with the idea of popping a couple more pills when he got home or just going straight back to sleep. Either way, he didn't like the emotions that had spilled during his session. The unexpected downpour of tears. He knew what he had purged was only the top layer. So much more wanted to spill out of every cell and it was too much.

Thick snowflakes fell from the sky and the world was a dirty acrylic white. Caleb shivered and realized the percs were wearing off. A hazy black dot in the distance shambled towards him with a familiar gait. Caleb rubbed his eyes, wondering if this was a lingering hallucination or flesh and bone.

The closer the figure came; the more anxiety swam around Caleb's gut. He wished the snow would rise up and consume him, pulling him deep beneath the frozen strata and annihilate his existence in a polar snap.

The mysterious man looked up and grinned. It was the fucking bootleg man out here in the snow, face nearly hidden in a trove of thick scarves, trying to sling his wares.

"Not right now." Caleb groaned with outstretched arms. A tear ran down his face, turning into ice before sliding off his cheek.

"You made a promise young man," the bootleg man was already digging into his bag and paused with pleading eyes. "Are you not a man of your word? Should I think of you as a liar? That's not a good quality to have at your age and would reflect poorly on your generation."

Caleb sighed, feeling the guilt wrap around him like a wet blanket. "No, I'm not a liar. I'm just going through a lot and you have a tendency to show up at the worst time. But I did make a promise. What you got?"

"I got something special. A rare find."

"Yeah, yeah, yeah, you have a foreign film or something like that?"

"Naw, something even better." The bootleg man pulled out a stack of VHS tapes that resembled black bricks inside of his hands.

"C'mon man. I don't have a VHS player. You might as well be giving me stone tablets in a dead language."

The bootleg man laughed and started coughing. He spit out a wad of mucus with the smallest amount of red. It stood out, contrasting against the snow's sparkling white surface like a dark blemish, an environmental anomaly.

Caleb thought about saying something, maybe even encouraging the old man to get checked out, but couldn't find the willpower to even try. Death was knocking, and who was he to stop it?

"I'm sure your parents have a VCR stored away somewhere? Maybe in the basement? It's only been what ten, fifteen, maybe twenty years since they stopped selling em at electronic stores?" The bootleg man paused, concerned by the passage of time and the revelation that technology had completely outgrown him. "Damn I'm getting old."

"It's freezing out here. I don't have time to play semantics with you and debate the great age of cinema. How much?"

"How much you got?"

"VHS tapes haven't gone up in value," Caleb dug around his pockets and fished out a ten-dollar bill. "How's this?"

"That would be perfect, young man."

The bootleg man placed the bill up to the sky, searching for the non-existent sun to see if it was counterfeit or not. Then he sniffed it before stuffing it inside his left pocket.

Caleb grabbed the VHS tapes, snow melting on impact. He hoped the bootleg man wasn't scamming him, but he really just wanted the interaction to end.

"You don't have a bag for this? You don't want these to get damaged."

"No, obviously I don't." Caleb's brow furrowed in three wavy lines. He shifted from side to side.

"Hold on, I got you. Gimme one second." He pulled out a balled-up plastic grocery bag out of his coat pocket and put the VHS tapes inside.

"Thanks."

"Nice doin' business with you. Tell me what you think about the tapes. I got a special feeling about these in particular."

"Alright. See ya."

Caleb walked home, hands growing numbs as he trudged through the snow with the bag slightly swinging like a pendulum. He considered walking past his home, walking through the bare streets, praying the snowplow from earlier would fishtail onto the sidewalk, take him out, and end his misery with an undeniable finality.

Who truly gave a shit about him? He didn't accomplish anything of note in the last 18 years and who was actually going to notice his art? Such a temporary band-aid for the mountain of grief knotted inside his heart.

The tears came back with a vengeance and this time he didn't bother wiping them away.

Sturdy

Fredo moved down the sidewalk with a purpose, and rubbed his hands together, blowing air into the cold palms. He stuffed these same hands into the pockets of his black and gold bomber jacket with a small Playboy bunny stitched on each cuff, and a black Supreme beanie covering his inked head. He sized up the pedestrians as he passed them, a sea of business suits, peacoats, goretex, bulky coats, sweats, eyes sucked into phone screens or staring off into space. He gauged their potential strengths and weaknesses, taking note of their strides and gait, visualizing imaginary situations where he would get the chance to invoke violence and put his hands to good use.

Images of yanking on a coat collar, breaking a jaw, cutting soft flesh with his knuckles, all rose to the forefront of his mind and he smiled at the success of the imagined assaults.

Everyone he passed looked away with slight fear and apprehension at his sheer size and the menacing energy dripping off his frame despite his smirk. He turned a corner and bumped into a skinny nigga with teeth almost too large for his mouth and a phone propped up on a windowsill.

"Watch where the fuck you're going, you dumb fuck. Don't you see I'm doing something important?" The skinny nigga adjusted his beanie and sneered at Fredo, unaffected by his size and stature.

"Who the fuck you talking to?" Fredo said, getting up in the nigga's face, close enough to smell his rank breath and the lingering scent of marijuana even in the cold.

"Talking to you, nigga. Witcho yoked up Incredible Hulk-looking ass." He spat on the ground defiantly.

Fredo laughed, admiring the coiled audacity of the young buck, but this type of behavior would get him smoked sooner than later.

"Fuck are you laughing at? I'm no joke and that's on gang."

"And what gang is that? What block you from?" Fredo asked as he pulled his Glock 41 out of his waistband like a magic wand. "Let me know so I can spin it."

Fear engulfed the skinny nigga's brown eyes, which became as wide as a doe's as he backed away, reaching for his phone in the distance. People kept walking, wanting no part of the altercation blooming on the pavement.

"You didn't answer my question," Fredo said.

"I'm not in a gang. I'm just trying to record this video. Get my clout up."

"I figured that. I'm sure you didn't realize that I'm cut from a different cloth. That I'm Insane."

"You're a Vice Lord?"

"Bingo. See I knew you were smart."

The skinny nigga gulped.

"Why don't you continue doing what you were doing before our conversation started?" Fredo asked, snatching the phone and watching a draft of the nigga dancing moments earlier.

"I mean..."

"Don't act shy now, bro. I see you dancing, trying to become viral. Let me see you dance."

"Listen, I'm sorry I was talking crazy. I ain't know you were gang..."

"More than a gang. I represent a corporation. Almighty Vicelord Nation, a legal entity that you've just had the pleasure of meeting."

"O-okay, can I go home now?"

"No, these are the short-term effects of fucking with me. Now, what was I saying about this little dance of yours? Does it have a name? Is it a challenge or something original?"

"It's called getting sturdy."

"Ohhhhhhhhh you were getting sturdy, but you sure aren't built that way. You young niggas come up with dumb shit everyday. Let me see. I'll record you and everything. I know the angles. Make you look like a star."

"What if I say no?"

"Did I say you had options in this situation? You're going to dance one way or another. Don't make me use my pole, bro." Fredo hit play on the song cued up on the phone and put his Glock away, ready for the impending show.

Lil Uzi Vert's song "Just Wanna Rock" played on the phone's speakers. Sweat broke out on the skinny nigga's forehead despite the cold temperature. He moved back to his original spot and kicked his leg back multiple times to the beat, shifted his weight, and hopped on a bent leg. His knees swept in and out in sync with the beat and then he hopped forward on all fours, long arms sweeping back and forth, running in place like a cheetah. He kicked his legs out to the side, did a 360-degree spin, and stopped.

"That's it?" Fredo said, unimpressed by the performance. "That's you getting sturdy?"

"Yeah, but I have 20K followers..."

"Do I look like I give two shits about how many goofies follow you on the internet?"

A white Tesla slowly pulled up, the window hummed down, revealing Nate who grinned as he brandished a Mini Draco with a newly applied switch. His eyes were bloodshot and glossy from staying out all night, cruising the streets, and smoking strong weed.

"What do we have here?" Nate asked, aiming the gun out the window sideways. "Don't you know this is a no fly zone?"

Fredo pushed the skinny nigga into the line of fire, took off running, and let off a couple of haphazard shots at the Tesla. Not caring if he hit his intended target, he picked up the pace, hoping his sprinting days would still pay dividends.

Pop. Pop. Pop. Pop. Pop. Pop. Pop. Pop. Pop.

He heard the distinct sound of bullets ripping through flesh, a window shattering, and wheels struggling to gain traction on the slushie asphalt. His heart beat like a Darbuka drum inside his chest.

These niggas aren't turning my ass into a meme. I'll tell you that.

Fredo reached the end of the street before he heard the car skirt off in the distance. This was one of the rare times he was grateful for the winter weather. He would have been done for if it wasn't for the shitty street conditions, brutal climate, and lack of snowplows in the area.

He dipped down the next street, pivoting into the syrupy shadows of any alleyway. Taking deep breaths through his nose and exhaling out of his mouth, he gripped his Glock, ready for war.

Cars passed by and Fredo's right foot fell asleep and he lost track of time before he dared venture back out of the shadows. He peeked back around the corner of the original street he fled from and saw a mini crowd formed around the skinny nigga from earlier. An ambulance pulled up as people recorded the gruesome sight on their phones.

He felt bad for fucking with the kid, thinking it would be a good lesson, but he had to do what he had to. Wolves prowled these streets and it was either eat or be eaten.

Fredo's phone vibrated in his pocket and his stomach grumbled.

God, I'm starving.

Fredo met Jasmine inside a Boba tea shop, wishing the food options were more substantial. She looked beautiful as she sat there with her legs crossed, wearing pink earmuffs and hot pink Cartier shades, sipping on a rosehip milk tea and scrolling through her phone. Internally, he shook himself out of his reverie, needing to focus on the job.

This is business bro. Get it together. Don't get mesmerized by her looks. That's rule number four.

Jasmine grinned when she looked up from her phone and saw the imposing figure standing over her. She stood, carefully moving around the table, and gave Fredo a tight hug.

"I'm happy you made it. So nice to meet you in real life."

Fredo took in the sweet fruity scent of her perfume and enjoyed feeling her warm body pressed against his own. Still, he didn't like the effect she had on him and his scattered concentration.

"Same. I hope you haven't been waiting too long."

"Nope, not at all," She glanced at the time on her phone. "You got here two minutes after our agreed time. Pretty prompt if you ask me."

"Thanks. I like the sunglasses by the way."

She smiled, showing her perfect teeth. "Thank you. These are one of my favorite pairs for real for real."

Fredo nodded, not wanting to get too far off track. "So I heard you want to collaborate?"

"Yeah, I feel like our services are complementary and if done right, could be lucrative as fuck."

"People tend to like my collection. Could I see a party favor?"

"Of course." Jasmine pulled out a birthday-themed gift bag with blue ribbons tied on the handle and pushed it across the table, taking another sip of her tea.

Fredo opened the bag and pulled out a black switch, inspecting the auto sear. It looked clean and functional. He was surprised the petite girl in front of him produced this with a 3D printer of all things.

"Color me impressed."

"Thanks. I take a lot of pride in my business and I feel validated when my customers are satisfied."

"As you should." Fredo handed the bag back over to Jasmine.

"Why are you looking like that?" Jasmine laughed.

"Like what?" Fredo asked, surprised by the flutter of butterflies in his stomach.

"Your face. You look like you're thinking so hard about something. Loosen up."

"I was just thinking this is a dangerous business you're in and you're so...delicate. How do you stay safe?"

Jasmine looked around the relatively empty shop and pulled open a portion of her coat, revealing her custom Glock.

"She who trusts men is one who carries water in a riddle."

"I don't know what that means, but that piece tells me everything. I would have never guessed you were packing heat. You look so innocent."

"Exactly, but looks can be deceiving and I use that to my advantage."

"A little demon with a brain."

Jasmine shrugged and sipped her boba tea.

"Let me ask you a hypothetical question..."

"What's up?" Jasmine said, genuinely curious.

"If you could take that pretty Glock of yours and you could shoot someone down with no repercussions, who would it be?" Fredo's brown eyes glimmered.

"Whoever killed my parents."

"No shit. You're cold-blooded, my nigga. I respect it."

"What about you? How did you phrase it...who would you shoot down?"

Fredo shrugged, staring into the distance, eyeing the pastries behind the counter. His stomach grumbled.

"C'mon nigga, this isn't fair. Answer the question. Who would you kill?" Jasmine wondered if he already had bodies, there was something strangely cold about him. His aura emanated artic levels of coldness. Like he wouldn't hesitate if it came down to it.

"The nigga who shot down my brother. Fucking G-D. Growth and development my ass." A wave of palpable anger boiled beneath the surface of his stoic demeanor and rippled across his face.

"Oh shit, I'm sorry about your brother's passing." Jasmine covered her mouth, eyes visibly pained by the news.

"Nothing to cry about and it ain't your fault. It's just the world we live in and the inner workings of the city. Comes with the territory."

Jasmine nodded, taking another sip of her milk tea, resisting the urge to trauma bond and connect over grief. She gently dabbed at her lips with a napkin.

Fredo could tell this girl genuinely cared and he couldn't tell why. He fought the compulsion to reach across the table, caress her cheek, and squeeze her hand.

"Let me grab something to eat real quick," Fredo said in an effort to collect himself.

Jasmine stood, gathered her things, and tucked a few items into her black Saint Laurent Matelasse Envelope bag with a gold chain hanging off her shoulder.

"I gotta go. I hate to be rushing off like this."

"No worries. I'm happy I was able to meet you in person and I'm sure we'll be seeing each other again."

"Oh yeah, you got my number. Don't be shy." Jasmine gave him a tight hug and blew him a kiss as she scrambled out of the shop with milk tea in hand.

The scent of pear, dewy honeysuckle, jasmine sambac, and cashmere woods lingered in the air. Fredo sat in silence for a moment before he made his way toward the counter and ordered a piece of sachertorte, salivating over the chocolate cake. After paying, he sat back down and took a bite from the fresh pastry.

Licking his lips, he wondered if the YSL bag she wore being black and gold was some sort of coincidence, sharing the same colors his gang proudly embraced, a synchronicity symbolizing things falling into place.

Fredo shrugged and took another bite, relishing the decadent cake and considered buying another slice for later. He cursed as he bit his tongue. Blood shimmered on the tip of his index finger, reflecting his face painted red with concern.

Quality Control

Pop. Pop. Pop.

Jasmine held the Glock or what she liked to refer to as her glocky steady in her soft hands, focusing her sights on the paper target in the distance. It was a display of Donald Trump in a blue suit with a red tie, sticking his tongue out obnoxiously. She channeled the energy of a Bengal tiger in her stance, slightly bending her knees, a fierce anger coiled in her upper body. Focusing on her rhythmic breath, she aimed for the center mass of the target in the distance, staring into the former president's dark gray eyes, and she pulled the trigger. One shot punctured his cheek, the next one tore through his Adam's apple and the third hit the space between his beady eyes.

This is for all the women you've shamed and objectified, you sick fuck. Trump this!

A keen sense of power surged through her athletic frame with every shot. Everything else in her life receded into the background and she was truly present in the moment. Completely immersed in *this* moment. This was her meditation, this was her peace. No man, woman, or animal would be able to stop her with a gun in her hand.

Her girlfriends always ragged on her, deeming the shooting range her second home away from home. But they weren't too far off the mark. She visited the shooting range at least three times a month, sometimes more and paid for the most expensive membership tier.

The shooting range was her temple, her sacred space. And she would protect this peace with every cell in her body.

Have to stay sharp. Don't allow your skills to atrophy and wither away bitch...stay ready.

She adjusted her safety glasses and pulled out a box of bullets from her jacket pocket. While reloading her gun, a light-skinned nigga with a nose ring and a strange birthmark on his cheek approached her with a sly grin. He wore a white hoodie with sweatpants and a gold Movado watch. She doubted the time was correct on his timepiece.

"Hey babygirl, you look like you know your way around a gun, but if I could offer one piece of advice...aim for the center of mass next time." He was nearly shouting the words, making sure she could hear him through her hearing protection lodged in both ears.

Did I miss the memo or was it international catcalling day?

"Did I ask for your unsolicited advice?" she asked.

"Can you speak up?" he said. "Can't hear you, babygirl."

She spoke up while gritting her teeth. "I'm not your fuckin babygirl, nigga. Now please leave me alone. No one wants to be hit on at a gun range. Get some sense."

He slowly pulled back one side of her hearing protection, revealing her pierced ear. Small gold hoops wrapped around her ear's helix.

"Well you know a nigga's gotta shoot his shot." He cheesed, revealing a set of absurdly white veneers. They were almost *too white*.

She pushed her hearing protection back over her ear and continued reloading her Glock, trying her best to ignore him and the rage bubbling inside her chest. No one else was around to intervene or step in.

"Why you gotta be like that? C'mon… look, I can help you with your shot. What do they say? There's always room for improvement."

Stay away from the evil and sing to it.

She finished loading the bullets into the magazine and watched him come up behind her, sliding his cold hands around her waist. She visibly cringed.

"Back up." She yelled, slapping his hands away. "I don't want you touching me, fuck nigga."

He laughed, gripping her hips and squeezing her love handles. She writhed away from his hands and moving off instinct pistol-whipped him across his forehead. His knees buckled and a nasty gash opened on his forehead like a third eye. Blood spilled down his white hoodie.

"You fucking thottie ass bitch," he said, gingerly touching his forehead and looking down at the blood coating his fingertips. "I-I'm going to shove my gun in your mouth and throat fuck you so hard you'll regret this for the rest of your life. You dumb cunt."

She took off like a bat out of hell, running out of the gun range as fast as possible, thankful she didn't bring a larger weapon case. The clerk waved as she hustled out the front door, not bothering to glance back behind her. Knowing she was on camera, she wondered how bad the scene looked. Would she get charged? Was that considered assault? How bad is a felony? She couldn't remember the specifics or the legalities, but she had no wish to do any real-time. That had to be self-defense, right? She was in danger or at least she thought so.

Jasmine maintained a clean record for 22 years and she wasn't going to let some pervy nigga who couldn't control his impulses ruin that. He deserved it, but still...she wondered if she overreacted.

Snap out of it, Jas, that man has no respect for women. No respect for boundaries. Nigga had it coming. And what would have happened if you didn't do anything? How far would he have gone?

She slid into the driver's seat of her car, put on her shades, checked herself out in the mirror, and took a deep breath. Her hands were shaking, and she had no idea how long. She wiped the sweat from her forehead, looked down at her blood-stained Glock in the passenger seat, and nodded before speeding off.

Now I have to clean this blood off my favorite Glock, fuck nigga.

I Spoke to the Devil in Chicago

Caleb emptied his pockets into a small scratched-up gray bin and stood behind two other senior students. He eyed Mr. Dawson who was sweating profusely. The black teacher wore a polka dot silk tie, rolled up sleeves, a gun hung from his waist, and he looked like he rather be doing anything else besides monitoring teenagers on a Wednesday morning for weapons.

Two long lines of teenagers fidgeting with their cellphones and complaining about the wait stood behind Caleb, eager to pass through the twin set of metal detectors and get on with their day.

Caleb hated the daily ritual, he hated the electronic gateway to a public high school education, and he resented the overt violation of his privacy. Despite the presence of the metal detectors and an uptick in security presence throughout the halls, students got caught every other week trying to bypass the system, sneak in a gun, a knife or some other weapon. The school faculty, parents, and local community were scared shitless of the idea of a school shooting happening or a gang war breaking out in the dead of winter.

It wasn't too far-fetched, especially with the massive number of baby-faced gang members walking through the hallways, throwing up sets, and contorting their fingers into strange shapes in an attempt to threaten the opps.

"You're good," Mr Dawson said, waving Caleb through. "Please pay attention and keep the line moving." Caleb gathered his belongings and headed to homeroom. The day passed by without any problems and he eventually made it to his favorite class—art.

His teacher, Miss Kerrigan, wore her fiery red hair in a loose ponytail, and rocked a tight-fitting kimono with orange osmanthus, autumn sakura, and red spider lilies printed on the silk fabric, which hugged her curves and served as the perfect representation of her quirky personality.

"Caleb, nice to see you. How are you doing?"

Caleb shrugged. "I'm okay."

"Awww you should smile more often, but I do have something that might cheer you up."

"What's that?"

"We got a large order of fresh art supplies in at four AM this morning. The same order that was delayed for months. You can finally get started on that painting you were talking about."

"Oh shit, that's what's up." Caleb covered his mouth, remembering where he was at. He tried to keep cussing to a minimum since his teacher hated it.

"Don't worry about it. We all slip up. It'll be our little secret."

Caleb nodded. He donned his thick headphones, putting out a clear signal to his classmates that he was in work mode and didn't want to be bothered. Turned on a Lil Tracy playlist with nothing but sad-ass bangers. He propped up his blank 8x10 stretched canvas on a janky wooden easel. Adjusting it multiple times until it stood still and could hold the weight of the canvas.

He picked up a green 3H charcoal pencil and got to work, loosely sketching the outline of an obscenely large head. Quick movements of his left hand. Following the nudge of his daimon muse, he continued following his intuition as he lightly added details to the sharp eyes and the mouth with two rows of jagged teeth, which turned into bullets.

Frustrated by a couple of small mistakes, Caleb erased the blunders with a gum eraser. He continued defining the abnormal face, completing the skinny nose, and mottled skin texture, when he was rocked by the feeling of déjà vu.

Did I see this face somewhere before? In a dream maybe?

A hand gripped his shoulder and Caleb almost leaped out of his chair.

"You okay, Caleb?" Miss Kerrigan asked, concerned.

He peeled back one headphone from his ear. "Yeah, I'm good. You know how I get when I'm in work mode. Complete immersion."

"Yeah, I know this all too well. Just wanted to say you're doing lovely work even though the material is dark."

"Dark's my forte."

Miss Kerrigan smiled as she moved on to the next student, ready to critique their work and offer some helpful advice. "Keep it up."

"Thanks, I will."

Caleb mixed a combination of blue oil paint with turpentine inside his paint tray. He pulled out a sable brush and applied a few strokes of vibrant blue to the canvas.

The bell rang, shocking his nervous system and activating a ball of anxiety in his stomach. He quickly cleaned up and put away his painting with the obscene face stuck inside his mind like a splinter, nagging him like a deranged psychopomp, dragging him back down into the depths of his depression.

Turning on the VCR was much easier than Caleb had originally anticipated. He followed the YouTube tutorial to the T and it took less than five minutes to figure out the archaic device. Just had to make sure the VCR he ordered off the internet wasn't a rip-off. He pushed a VHS tape into the slot and there was a soft pull, which caught Caleb off guard. The tape was swallowed by the dark recess.

The VCR whirred, clicked, and sounded like something was being loaded. Caleb felt himself growing impatient and scrolled through his phone. He had already watched five videos by the time his attention snapped back to the TV when a dark shade of green filled the screen and there was a prominent FBI piracy warning displayed. He laughed, imagining the bootleg man getting swarmed by a group of men in suits, guns pointed at his head.

Shit must be serious.

He sipped on a pop, relishing the soft burn of the drink and threw back a perc, readying himself for some fun. A soft static buzz filled the room and the screen showed jagged lines of distortion moving in purple waves. A blurry image came into a soft hazy focus and Caleb was almost disturbed by the lack of picture quality. He couldn't believe people used to live like *this*. No wonder old folks are so bitter. They've been missing out.

A close-up of a green plant. Something blurry sticking out of the waxy skin similar to needles. The videographer zoomed out, revealing a wet cactus, glochids poking out of the saguaro like a malignant mass of bristling constellations. The cactus *moved* or to be more accurate, multiple *parts* were moving. It had a short tail, small claws protruding from its ribs, and it was hunched over kind of like a mal-adjusted monkey. A small wet gash opened in the center of the cactus, resembling a crooked mouth, and it screamed.

Caleb covered his ears and scrambled for the remote. His head was pounding, unable to decipher the plant's torturous language. He almost broke the remote, bashing the volume button down, and hit stop on the VCR. The machine whirred and buzzed in response. The screen turned black.

He hit eject.

Heart racing.

Hands sweaty.

Ceiling fan spinning overhead.

That shit had to be fake, right? Or maybe it was staged? Special effects couldn't be that good back in the day, or could they?

There was an air of authenticity about the cactus that he couldn't deny. The perc didn't even kick in yet and Caleb felt like he was tripping on shrooms. Did he really just witness a cactus monkey or was this an elaborate prank? Some sort of sick joke? He knew they had good effects back in the 80s, especially in films like *Alien, The Thing, and the Fly*. But this felt *real*. He observed animals and humans throughout his 18 years on this Earth and whatever that thing was, was certainly *breathing*...

Caleb thought about running up on the bootleg man and punching him in the gut, placing his shaky hands around the man's scrawny neck and making him beg for mercy.

The room shifted as if a mental switch had been flipped on and his anger slowly dissipated. The perc had finally kicked in. A small white godsend flowing through his bloodstream, cradling him in a dreamlike softness, keeping the dark thoughts and that haunting face from his painting at bay, and his traumatic memories from spilling over into the present.

Caleb took the VHS tape and tossed it in the trash. He briefly considered lighting the whole thing on fire, ready to embrace the warmth and destruction.

Don't do all that. You don't need the smoke alarm going off and a firetruck coming through. Whole block would be on my ass.

The perc calmed his frayed nerves and erased the thoughts from his mind entirely.

Zen.

That was the state he had reached. The shit Buddhist monks and transcendental meditation specialists lectured about. He was there, zeroed in the center of it all. Human consciousness bubbling over in a shitty house in Austin, Chicago.

Caleb grabbed another tape, this one saying PROJECT BULLET BABY along the side in faded writing, but images of that cactus mouth broke through the surface of his consciousness, and he put the VHS back down. He slid some wireless headphones into his ears and put on a playlist of XXXtentacion's saddest songs. He started out with "Jocelyn Flores" since he resonated with the grief and pain embedded into the vocals.

Curiosity nagged at him and he couldn't help but pick up the tape and slide it into the slot. He had to find out what the hell the mysterious title meant. It was eating at him.

He hit play on the VCR and took another sip of his pop, relishing the carbonated burn running down his chest.

The screen was dark and fuzzy, crackling and popping.

Here.

We.

Go.

He finished the pop and tossed it in the trash can, hoping the leftover fluid would ruin the VHS tape forever. The VCR whirred, and something clicked. A U.S. Government logo flashed on the screen with the word classified in small letters. Faded into black and was replaced by the sound of soft static waves and the camera shook as if the operator had a case of tremors.

There was a case of guns on a beach, gleaming underneath a splash of moonlight. Bullets embedded in the sand like washed-up debris. Shapes churned in the water, shadows etched into the ocean.

The letter B flashed on the screen.

Gunfire rattled off in the distance. Booming shots fired from the mouth of an unknown automatic weapon. It became a steady rhythm of gunfire building into a crescendo of violence.

Something akin to a grin flashed on the screen and Caleb felt a lump of anxiety in his gut and the hairs on the back of his neck stood at attention. Something was clearly wrong, but he couldn't take his eyes off the screen. They were fixated on the found footage and his body was deadweight, limbs nearly paralyzed by the drugs flowing through his system.

A static screech filled the room and the dim outline of a face pushed against the constraints of the flat-screen TV mounted on the wall, the same face he was painting in art class. Caleb tried to will himself towards the remote, but his body felt like it was full of lead. He was going to be forced to see this through to the end.

Caleb's mouth slowly moved and the words "Bullet Tooth" spilled out. He didn't know why he said that or where the thought even came from. It was almost as if something was willing him to say the words.

"Bullet Tooth."

Small bullets pushed their way out of the sand and ripped through the screen, plopping down on the floor. Vibrating and buzzing on the carpet.

Caleb would have pissed himself if it wasn't for the percs numbing his bladder. The bullets vibrated and cracked open like golden eggs. Bones sprouted out of the bullets like a white fungus. It grew 6 feet tall, forming the rough outline of a human figure. Tight musculature and connective tissues grew out of the bones like ivy.

Get up. Get the fuck up, he yelled at his slumped body.

His right hand twitched and he considered that a win. He forced it forward, pricks of pain shooting throughout his palm. His hand clasped the remote like a life raft and he finally shut the TV off. To his astonishment, the physical aberration continued growing.

Its *head,* if you could call it that, was huge, almost too big for its lean muscular body. Adam's apple throbbing in its throat. Nipples popped out of his broad chest and a big dick sprouted in between its legs. Cold eyes filled both eye sockets with a wet glistening *pop.*

The monstrosity grinned, revealing a set of bullets lodged in its black gums instead of teeth. It smelled like charred meat, turmeric, bird shit, and a hint of sulfur.

It turned its sights on Caleb, still sitting on the floor.

Caleb panicked while the monstrosity sauntered towards him, taking jerky steps, becoming accustomed to the physical vessel it inhabited. His throat was closing up and Caleb worried that he might pass out. Maybe it was time he kicked his perc habit once and for all and seek out rehab or a church.

Bullet Tooth wrapped its newly born hand around Caleb's neck, thumbing the trachea and giving it a soft squeeze. Drool dripped down its pointed chin.

"Why did you call me, child?" Bullet Tooth's voice buzzed with electricity and his facial features shifted erratically, mimicking Caleb's before wavering into new territory. His nose bridge elongated, cheek bones became more defined, dimples appeared and disappeared on his volatile physiognomy.

Caleb struggled to breathe but managed to answer the question.

"I didn't."

"Don't lie. I heard you clearly say my name, not once, but repeatedly, and you *chose* to play the video. You summoned me back into this 3D realm. I'm sorry your soft brain can only comprehend so much, but I'm here to stay and I plan on having some fun."

"I-I didn't mean to say your name and I had no idea what I was doing. I swear... I bought these tapes off the bootleg man."

"They never do, do they? Don't worry yourself, child. Just know that you are capable of so much more than you realize. You are capable of inflicting so much violence, you have the potential to cause so much pain. You can get rid of that depression you harbor once and for all with a gun. I'm not speaking of suicide mind you, but something far greater."

"Like what?" Caleb wasn't sure if something had finally cracked inside his delicate mind, and these were the consequences of all the pills he had popped throughout his short life or if this was some part of reality that had been conveniently hidden away from him.

"It starts with a gun. It always does. You humans can't live without violence. I feel so much pain and anguish inside of you, it's becoming unbearable. Avenge your friend my child. Embrace that anger, channel it into something *constructive*, something cathartic. This too is art."

Bullet Tooth's words were soothing and hypnotic. They felt like something Caleb should seriously consider, a path he should take. And how did he know about his artistic talents? This discovery didn't disturb him, but he felt like the statement should have rattled him.

"I'll think about it."

Bullet Tooth laughed and strolled towards the bedroom door.

"Where are you going?" Caleb asked, not wanting him to leave.

"Into the world, my child. There are new guns, new weapons of mass destruction. People who could use my guidance within the asphalt. They need me."

"What about me?" Caleb couldn't believe himself. Why was he speaking to this monstrosity as if he was an old friend or a prominent figurehead of authority?

"Don't worry. I have not abandoned you like your father, your school, your ancestors or your government...I could go on for days. You brought me back into this world. I thank you for that, but your hands might as well be doused in the blood of those about to be slaughtered. Call my name once you make up your mind. I have no patience for indecisiveness."

Caleb nodded and Bullet Tooth exited his room. Moments later, he heard the front door open and shut.

What the hell just happened?

He questioned his sanity and his reality, but the VHS tape was still real, and the scent of sulfur was thick in the air. Bullet Tooth was real and was out there, roaming the streets of Chicago.

Caleb got up and popped a handful of pills, searching for the sweet embrace of oblivion underneath his tears as he pondered Bullet Tooth's proposition playing over and over inside his head like an ear worm.

The Origins of an Insane Vice Lord

The first time Fredo held a gun was at the tender age of 11. He was scared shitless, and his small hands shook like two pups left to fend for themselves in the cold. He remembered his older brother Miguel roasting him outside with a black bandana hanging out of his back pocket. The sun beamed down aggressively, and everything had a soft haze.

"Come on, pussy. It's just a gun," his brother displayed the burner as if it was a harmless toy. "And the safety's on... you don't want to be like your big bro?"

Fredo accepted the gun, feeling as if it was a steel death sentence passed down to him. A generational curse waiting to happen. He remembered his chest feeling tight and the gun feeling like a live wire in his hand. He wanted nothing to do with it. Shooting people in videogames was cool mainly because it was harmless, but he worried his whole world would disintegrate if he pulled the trigger. There were no respawns in real life.

His brother was a Gangster Disciple, initiated into the gang at the age of 12. Fredo never learned what he did to become a member, but he saw the transformation in his brother's once kind eyes, and his overall aura screamed danger from that day forward. The softness had faded completely and was replaced by a frigid cold that had Fredo treading lightly around him.

The crazy thing is Fredo followed in his brother's footsteps a couple of years later, but he switched sides and joined the Insane Vice Lords after learning about a GD snitching on his big bro. He used to look up to them, sharing blunts and liquor even going as so far to rocking a fitted White Sox hat and running random errands for them. It made him sick to his stomach when he discovered the identity of the rat.

Fredo hunted the goofy down when he got older, gained mass, and put on muscle. He couldn't let it go. He tried forgiveness, he tried attending church, he tried channeling all of his rage into a short-lived boxing career, but it wasn't enough. Murder was the only viable option and the penultimate answer he was seeking.

The gangster he hunted had become a shell of his former self, sleeping on couches and selling scrap metal and copper to make a living if you could call it that.

Fredo pulled off his first kill at the age of 17 with a Sig Sauer P38. It wasn't in the best condition, but it got the job done. The killing act had felt like a fever dream, some parts still difficult for Fredo to fully recall.

The doorknob was covered in a sticky film and Fredo managed to walk inside the apartment with no issue. His breathing was somewhat labored in his balaclava, but he made due. He couldn't believe the negligence of the nigga, leaving his front door unlocked.

Moving quietly, he found the motherfucker passed out on the couch, surrounded by containers of Chinese takeout and half-smoked joints. *Seinfeld* was blaring on the TV in the living room, drowning the world outside the apartment. Elaine and Jerry stared at George, dumbfounded by his Goretex coat. The nigga was dripped out from head to toe.

Fredo aimed his gun at the snitch's head, half expecting his hands to shake or someone to pop out of the bathroom dramatically, but nothing happened. Fredo pulled the trigger and watched as the bullet ripped through the nigga's head, blood splattering the couch. And just like that, it was over.

Fredo quickly left, taking the fire escape, barely feeling tethered to the reality of the act he just carried out. Emotions swam around his gut like eels, but he tried to disconnect as he hurried down the steps and dipped into an alleyway to freedom. He hung low for a couple of months before returning to work, running guns.

Guns induced fear in him at first, but slowly he had become desensitized to weapons and fell in love with artillery. He worked his way up the ranks of the Insane Vice Lords and managed to become the go-to-arms dealer for his crew.

Guns had become his life and they consumed him. He couldn't imagine his life being any different. There was a high demand in the city for guns and he provided an ample supply in turn keeping his pockets fat and healthy.

His second love was money, but still, there was one void that couldn't be fulfilled. His brother Miguel was locked up in state prison, doing 20 years for drug trafficking. He had only served six of those years, but it killed Fredo knowing his brother, his blood was suffering. Being a diligent brother, he put money on his books, phoning certain people behind bars and pulled a couple favors to make sure his brother was straight.

Fredo was aggressive, but he was smart, discreet, and above all else careful. He tied up his loose ends and wasn't scared to go the extra mile. Couldn't be any help to his brother if he was locked up too.

Still, the fear and paranoia followed him everywhere he went like a rabid dog. He lifted weights and boxed to keep the demons at bay. It helped, but it wasn't a solution, more like a waterproof bandage.

Yet here he was with a Glock shoved in the back of his waistline, nestled at the base of his spine. He walked towards the warehouse with caution, but relaxed once he saw a shit-ton of people standing outside. Rap music grew louder, the closer he approached.

Women were dressed in tight revealing outfits, while a portion of the men wore baggy clothes posturing as gangsters. The other portion of men were dressed like Playboi Carti clones. Tight leather pants, buckles, piercings, light make-up. Black goths. Black vamps. He snickered, thinking about trying a couple of them just for fun. Still, he didn't want to cause a commotion. He was here for business and maybe a little bit of fun.

He didn't know what to think about the vamps. He kept it moving, looking for his client Udom, a thai nigga. He was supposed to be dressed in a polo shirt, and had a thick black mustache. Should be easy to spot amongst this crowd.

Someone with a big ass head bumped into Fredo. It felt a bit aggressive, and he considered reacting, pulling out his Glock and showing this nigga he wasn't anything sweet. He managed to swallow the anger down and headed towards the entrance, brushing the collision off, chalking it up to an accident. Still, something about the interaction made him uneasy.

Security stood outside the doors, but didn't give two shits and let him inside with no issue. He headed towards the bar, watching the strobe lights move around the room, dousing dancers in vibrant colors. It was a huge open space, packed to the brim with glistening bodies. A few women looked appetizing, and he considered making a move, but he reminded himself about the mission at hand.

He paid for a pale ale, found an open spot at the bar and leaned back against the counter. He surveyed the party, searching for his client in the crowd. Pulled out his phone and sent a "where u at?" text.

This nigga better not be playing games because I'm not the one.

A text came through with a surprising quickness. "In the middle of the dancefloor."

Fredo's neck grew tense. He wanted to punch something or somebody. He needed a release...

Who acts like this? Did this motherfucker not have any decency? Here I am going to this party just like he wanted and he's too busy dancing.

"I'm by the bar. Can you come over here, bro?"

"In a minute. Let me wrap something up. I appreciate you coming out. *fist emoji*"

"Np."

Fredo downed the rest of his beer and saw the weird nigga with the big ass head grinding on a Latina with a ponytail and tattoos. He wondered what this man's deal was and how did he pull a dime like that?

He shrugged.

There's someone for everyone.

What Would Virgil Do?

Jasmine didn't know why she was going to the party, but she couldn't pass up a fashion opportunity. Social obligations maybe... She could just binge-watch TV, lay up in bed and smoke a blunt, but she knew she could get more exposure which meant more followers, more sponsorships, more money, and more guns. Never could have enough guns.

She stared in the bathroom mirror, fixing her bangs and struggling to get her magnetic eyelashes to stick properly without looking like some insect crawling out of her eyes. Blowing air out of her nostrils, she changed the song on her portable speaker from the soft love songs of Maxwell to Dom Kennedy's "Locals Only."

"That right," she bopped to the song, swaying her body from side to side. She considered going live on social media, but she was enjoying her time alone, relishing the momentary bout of solitude.

She moved closer to the mirror, getting a better look at the red outline of a heart tatted below her left eye. It looked cute, but it was beginning to fade. She made a mental note to schedule an appointment to get the ink freshened up.

Can't be looking crazy out here.

Moving into her walk-in closet, she admired her shoe collection, and ran her fingers along the clothes hanging to the right of her. She couldn't believe she accumulated all of these clothes in such a short amount of time. Just this time last winter, she was struggling to make rent, but she always gambled on herself and she was winning in spades.

She tried on a couple of dresses, admiring herself in the full-length mirror, but the fashion choices didn't *feel* right to her. Filling her left cheek with a bubble of air, she stood there thinking.

What would Virgil do?

Inside her chest, she felt a pang of sadness strike a chord and grief wormed its way up her throat. She wished he was still alive. He was one of her favorite designers and he had accomplished so much, especially as a black man in a space saturated with so many white people. And it didn't hurt how much his clothes brought her attention and clout.

"Off-White it is," she said, happy to have made a firm fashion decision. A weight melted off her shoulders and she pulled a black and white shirt off the hanger displaying a portrait of Mona Lisa with cursive writing beneath it. She pulled out a matching black skirt, fishnets, and tall black platform boots.

She put on the outfit, stood in front of the mirror, and snapped a couple of photos. Doing a quick edit with an app, she posted one online with the address of the underground party.

While waiting for her girlfriends to come scoop her up, she poured herself a generous shot of henny and tossed it back. It burned all the way down to her esophagus, but she loved it. Made her feel alive. It was going to be a good night.

Her friend Ashley pulled up with Tatiana and Nicole in an orange Audi A6. Jasmine slid in the backseat, already feeling the communal energy building between the girls.

"Yassss bitch," Ashley turned back towards Jasmine. "You look snatched."

"I know right?" Jasmine laughed.

"You look great," Nicole said.

Tatiana was busy texting someone, face awash in a digital glow thanks to her phone in hand.

"Earth to Tati," Jasmine waved her manicured hands. "Who you texting?"

"Rob."

Everyone rolled their eyes and sighed in unison. "I thought you dropped that nigga?"

"Shit, I thought I did too, but look at what I'm doing."

"Is he coming to the party?"

"He's acting funny. I have no idea, but I'm trying to convince his dumbass. I invited him last week, but you know how he is..."

"What happened to slut era?" Jasmine asked.

"That era's cancelled," Tatiana waved her off and returned to her phone.

"A dog's tail will never straighten out," Jasmine said, shaking her head.

"Ain't that the truth," Ashley said.

"Whatever," Tatiana said.

Jasmine shrugged, knowing it was a useless cause. Tati was going to do what Tati wanted to do at the end of the day. No one could tell her a damn thing or make her change her mind. She was stubborn, but that was her girl and she was going to support her regardless.

Ashley turned up the radio, singing along to Jack Harlow's "First Class."

"That white boy is overrated," Nicole said.

"He's cute though." Tatiana said, chiming in from the back.

"Couldn't be me, but I do like his music," Jasmine said.

Ashley commanded the girls in the car. "Everyone shut up and just enjoy the song."

Jasmine thought about the guy she pistol-whipped and wondered if he would show up at the party. She kicked herself for not bringing a gun and realized she doxxed herself with the social media post from her earlier. It was stupid and she felt ten times more vulnerable. Without a gun on her person, she felt small, all too human, and she hated that with a passion.

She tried to shake it off, but the paranoia was beginning to sink in. She needed another drink asap. What she had earlier wasn't doing the trick and she didn't want to stay hardwired into this loop of negativity and fear. It wasn't her style or her vibe.

"You okay, Jas?" Tatiana said, staring at Jasmine while texts flooded her phone's screen.

"Y-yeah, I'm good. I was just thinking."

"Don't think too hard now. It doesn't suit you. Plus, you don't want wrinkles forming early."

Jasmine lightly shoved Tatiana, forcing laughter and a smile on her face. "I told you I'm good, bitch."

"Alright, alright. We're here."

The girls hopped out the car and stepped into the cold night air. The warehouse was huge and there was a ton of people outside smoking weed and sharing drinks.

"Oh this is wild," Jasmine said, perking up as they entered the party.

The interior was huge and massive throngs of people were dancing to the music pouring out the speakers. The bar was packed and they made their way over, using their looks to get a bartender's attention who was sporting a frohawk. They ordered shots of henny and threw it back immediately. And they repeated this ritual two more times.

Moving to the dance floor, Jasmine noticed her body becoming nice and warm. She bent over and twerked to Doja Cat's "Streets." Nicole smacked her ass playfully.

"Are you getting video of this?" Jasmine asked, not missing a note and her head broke out in a thin sweat.

Tatiana held her phone out, recording Jasmine's sensual movements. "You know I got you, girl."

Jasmine was so used to documenting every aspect of her life for the internet, it was second nature at this point. It used to make her uncomfortable, trying to look perfect for strangers online, but it became liberating. She didn't mind the trolls, the good and bad comments or the fraction of fame she had amassed. Overtime, she embraced the term "influencer" and used the power to the best of her ability and felt like she was doing good in the world and spreading awareness.

Ashley and Nicole were talking to two men in a flirtatious manner, becoming consumed in conversation and light touches. Tatiana headed off in search of the bathroom and Jasmine found herself bopping by her lonesome.

A racially ambiguous man with a big ass head, wearing shades and a button-up shirt, grinned, revealing a shark grill in his mouth. Light reflected off his fronts like a lighthouse, nearly blinding Jasmine.

She shielded her eyes with her hand. "What the hell."

He moved into her personal bubble, grabbing Jasmine's bedazzled gun chain hanging off her neck in his hand. "Where'd you get this from? Etsy?"

"Nigga back up, do these look fake? And have you heard of boundaries?"

He took a step back. "My bad. I was compelled to touch the chain. It's marvelous. Must be worth a lot of money."

"Thanks," she was already growing tired of this exchange, wishing she had taken another shot of henny instead of being caught in the open by this motherfucker.

"How are you enjoying the party?" He asked, pulling a device out of his pocket. It was hard to see in the dim lighting of the warehouse.

"It's cool, I guess." She crossed her arms.

"Why do they call this an underground party? I used to party in the catacombs in Paris, drink champagne in bunkers, and indulge in narcotics at basement parties. This," he motioned his hands around. "This is false advertising. This is a mockery. Pan would be rolling in his grave."

"Pan? You talking about the horny goat dude with flutes hopping around the forest?"

"Yeah the horny goat dude."

"I don't know what to tell you man," she shrugged. "A party's a party."

He grabbed her chain again, placing the diamond tester next to it, watching the meter slowly moving to the right.

Jasmine looked at him, feeling like she was under some divine test even though she wouldn't be caught dead wearing fake jewelry or fake designer.

What was wrong with men and their lack of boundaries? I'm like a magnet for these losers.

The light on the diamond tester moved into the yellow and three bars of red. It beeped loudly.

"You passed."

"We're real out here. Nothing fake about me."

"Noted."

The man with the oversized head, slipped into a pocket of bodies and disappeared into the crowd.

What the fuck just happened? What is wrong with men? You know what, it's not my burden to carry. I need to find the girls and get a fresh shot of henny. Get my mind right.

A large group of people hovered around someone on the dancefloor, snapping photos and causing a small commotion. Jasmine was curious so she moved in closer, trying to get a better look at the source.

Tatiana tapped her shoulder. "Hey where have you been? I've been looking all over. Almost made me call the cops"

"Don't be dramatic. I've been dealing with broke niggas. What's going on?"

"Big Poliano is here. People are going crazy."

"Big Poliano! I love his mixtape Pole Talk. Nothing but fire."

"Me too, girl."

Jasmine squeezed in between a few people, saying excuse me as she moved closer. Big Poliano had on a number of ridiculous chains hanging down to his gut poking out of a vintage Chrome Hearts hoodie, Chrome Hearts leather fatigue cargo pants secured with a Gucci belt, and Yeezy 950 pirate boots. A huge entourage of gang members surrounded him like a military unit as phone cameras flashed. He was eating up the attention, loving every bit of it.

Big Poliano locked eyes with Jasmine, licking his thick lips. He approached her slowly and she grew nervous.

Whatever is written on the forehead is always seen.

"Hey girl, what's your name? You look familiar like I've seen you before."

"Jasmine."

"Jasmine, Jasmine, Jasmine," he stroked his beard, thinking. "Oh shit, you're the fine ass girl with the gun collection. Your pictures don't do you justice."

"Thanks."

"I wish you would stop with all that feminist shit. It's exhausting. Let a nigga be a nigga in peace."

"No, it's not exhausting, nigga," Jasmine crossed her arms. "It's a way of life and I'm not stopping just cuz you don't like it."

"Slow down girl. I don't want any smoke. I actually wanted to invite you to a music video shoot. It'll be fun and I think you might add some much-needed flavor to the mix."

"Really?"

"Yeah I'm serious. Take down my number and I'll have my people text you the addy."

Jasmine took down the number in her phone despite feeling pissy and defensive. This was a good business opportunity, and this could potentially expand her platform and her fanbase. She was hoping this wasn't some roundabout way of him trying to get in her pants because she wasn't anyone's hoe.

"It was nice meeting you Jasmine. And if you pull up to the shoot maybe you can educate me on some of that feminist shit too."

"I can't say the same, but I'll be there."

"Big bet."

Big Poliano posed for pictures with other fans and Tatiana popped back out of the woodwork.

"I can't believe you just got invited to Big Poliano's video. That shit is bananas. You got the juice, girl."

"I guess."

"Don't be like that, Jas. Let's find Nicole and Ashley and get some more henny in you. What do we always say?"

"Hennything's possible."

Perky's Calling

"Come on, nigga. It's a party. You need to get out the house. Don't make me come kidnap you." Caleb's friend Rockit had trap music playing in the background and the sound of a lighter flicked.

"Alright nigga, I'll come. What's the dress code?"

"Dress code? Whatever the hell you want, twin."

"I don't know why you always have to call me twin. I feel like it's going to fall out of favor six months from now. Nigga, friend, twin, it's all interchangeable."

"Damn, nigga, I know you're depressed, but I didn't know you were the slang police. The slang solicitor, the slang sergeant ass lookin nigga."

"Alright, alright, I'm coming. Just be outside in 45."

"Bet."

Rockit pulled up in his Nissan Altima, tires crushing the snow underneath its tread. The bass was booming and Lil Durk blasted out the speakers.

Caleb hopped in the passenger seat, already regretting his choice to leave the house and be social. He was growing to hate being outside.

"Why you looking depressed, twin?"

"It's cuz I am depressed, *twin*."

"Don't worry, we'll get some drinks in you. Maybe you'll get lucky and get some pussy tonight. You know the thotties are out in full force."

Caleb could care less about getting some pussy, let alone humanity at this point, but he kept those thoughts to himself. He was worried he was becoming a misanthrope and falling out of touch with everything around him. But it felt completely out of his control and no one seemed to understand how his internal world was slowly unraveling one thread at a time.

"We'll see."

Rockit turned the music up and pulled an envelope from behind the sun visor. He opened it and jiggled out two pills.

"What's that," Caleb asked.

"Your favorite, you pill head. Don't turn into Famous Dex on me."

"Thanks, and I promise you I will never be tweakin like that nigga." Caleb dry swallowed the pills, relieved. "I knew the perky's were calling my name."

Rockit cruised down street after street, lights towering overhead like denizens of another dimension, looking down on them. Caleb enjoyed the warmth radiating from the air vents, considered going to sleep, and squeezing in a nap.

Rockit dug around the backseat while simultaneously driving and pulled out an unlabeled bottle of vodka.

"Take a sip of this, twin."

Caleb took a small sip and scrunched his face up as the warm liquor burned down his chest.

"You alright." Rockit said with a devilish grin on his face, taking the liquor back as he slowed to a stop at a red light.

"Where'd you get this shit from? A bum?"

"Naw, but don't worry about it," Rockit took a much bigger shot. "Just know it gets the job done."

Caleb laughed as his friend's face mirrored his own, looking visibly disgusted by the taste.

Rockit cranked the volume up, bobbing his head to FBG Duck's "Dead Bitches." Caleb joined in, nodding his head to the dark bass, but once the violent lyrics seeped into his conscious mind, drawing up images of Park's ravaged body, the iceberg of grief inside his gut ruptured. He stopped nodding and stared out the window, wiped away a tear, and watched the lights pass by.

"You alright?"

"Yeah, I'm fine," Caleb lied, not feeling in the mood to explain himself. He didn't want to kill the vibe and fuck up the night especially since Rockit was already in high spirits.

Rockit changed the song a couple times, settling on the Weeknd's "Reminder." Caleb eased into the song, living by the doctrine of fake it till you make it. Maybe if he forced his body to enjoy the music, maybe his brain would follow.

His friend became more animated, singing along to the toxic lyrics loud as hell, trying to pump Caleb up. Caleb grinned, appreciating Rockit's alcohol-fueled efforts to lift him out of his funk.

"We're here, twin." Rockit said parking haphazardly outside the warehouse. A ton of cars were parked at crazy angles and faint music bled outside the entrance.

"Looks litty." Caleb said, feeling a faint rush of excitement grow in his chest. The electricity in the night's air was undeniable.

"That's the Caleb I know," Rockit hit Caleb's chest lightly.

It was cold as hell so they shuffled through the snow without coats, rushing to the small line outside. They got inside with no problems whatsoever.

The interior of the warehouse was massive and it seemed like there were hundreds of people inside. Shit had to be a fire hazard, but Caleb was sure someone's palms were greased to keep this party going without interruption.

"Let's get some drinks," Rockit suggested.

"Yeah," Caleb said, already growing weary of the amount of people packed into the warehouse. Strobe lights moved over the crowd, highlighting the glistening bodies dancing. They looked like balls of flesh, packed into the space.

"Hey man, take a breath," Rockit wrapped his arm around Caleb, walking towards the bar. "Nothing bad's going to happen. I promise. It's just a party, twin."

"I got you. And I appreciate it. It's been a rough week. I feel like I've been seeing *things*."

"What type of things?" Rockit looked concerned.

Caleb felt like he spoke too soon and didn't want his friend thinking he belonged in the looney bin. "Don't worry about it. I had some bad pills I think."

"Oh okay. Make sure you ain't overdoing the pills. Shit can fuck you up. And speaking of getting fucked up, we got alcohol on deck."

Caleb smiled, doing his best to feign excitement for the night ahead. Internally, he felt terrible. The depression was always present like a hump in his back, trying to crush him under its emotional weight, sucking all the color and vibrancy from his life, leaving a gray vacuum behind.

One of the bartenders with a frohawk waved Rockit over and dapped him up. "Aye my nigga, glad you could make it."

"You making good money?"

"Tips lookin crazy. It's gonna be a good ass night. Whatchu you two want?"

"Whatever's going to get us right. And make my nigga Caleb's drink extra strong. He needs it."

"Bet."

"I thought we were going to take it slow?" Caleb said, worried about the depression seeping back in. He thought of depression as a ghost, something no one else could see except you. It knows you better than yourself, a shadow of a shadow haunting you in the most intimate way possible.

"C'mon, twin. It's the weekend. You have to loosen up. Get that darkness out of your system."

Caleb nodded despite the uneasy feeling growing inside his gut. He shoved it away, telling himself to just have a good time for once.

They threw back two shots and Caleb knew he was going to be floating in another universe pretty soon.

"Hey I'm going to take a piss," Rockit said. "I'll be right back. Try to talk to one of these hoes and get a number. Cheer yourself up while I'm gone."

Caleb moved back into the outskirts of the party, not wanting to be seen. He spotted some cute girls glancing at him. It made him uncomfortable and nervous. He wasn't sure if they were criticizing his fit or were showing interest. His head swam slightly, and he just wanted to disappear through a non-existent black hole.

For some reason, he remembered the augural image of Bullet Tooth in his bedroom, sprouting out of the bullets like a nightmare coming to fruition. He attributed the episode to the percs being bad, throwing that bottle in the trash that same night. The next day he asked the plug about it, but he just shrugged, playing dumb or being completely clueless to the situation.

"Shit happens. It is what is. What you want me to do about it? Can't go back in time."

Caleb purchased more pills despite the bad trip, but he couldn't shake that image burned into his mind. Was it possible that Bullet Tooth was real? And what was the likelihood that he channeled the thing into his painting? He knew he had a potent imagination, but this was something tangible. That monstrosity smelled like sulfur and the horrible scent lingered in the air the next day.

He had tossed the tapes in the trash, making sure there was no way someone else would have to witness that bullshit or even deal with that foul thing called Bullet Tooth. His grandma would have called those VHS tapes the devil and he wouldn't disagree.

A man with an oversized head and a gleaming grill tapped him on the shoulder, bringing Caleb back to reality, back to the party. He wished he approached the girls instead of having to deal with this funny-looking motherfucker. There was an air of familiarity about him, but Caleb couldn't quite place his mottled face.

"What's up," Caleb said, initiating the conversation.

"Nothing much. Just wanted to say hey. You looked a little lost. My name's Brian."

Caleb dapped him up and cringed, feeling a sweaty slime come off his palms. He wiped his hands on his pants discreetly as possible, wondering what type of nasty shit this nigga was into.

"I'm Caleb."

"You look familiar. Aren't you Park's best friend?"

"Yeah, do I know you?" Caleb wondered if he was a Black Disciple or affiliated with another gang, but he didn't look like he banged.

"No, but I get around. Let's just say niggas know about me."

Caleb nodded, not understanding the point of this conversation or where it was going. And why the hell was Rockit taking so long in the restroom?

"Can I ask you something? I mean I don't want to offend you or anything. I know some people are sensitive especially in this particular day and age."

"Go ahead," Caleb said, genuinely curious what this random nigga had to say. And why did he speak like that? Particular day and age...

"How did you let that nigga get away with shooting your brother like that? Doesn't that fuck with you? Doesn't that eat away at your soul at night? I mean if it was me, I would've slid already. Got revenge."

Caleb was stunned, speechless.

The big-headed man draped his arm around Caleb's shoulders, bringing him in closer, the harsh smell of liquor pouring off his breath in waves. "Listen I know who did it or least I'm pretty sure. It's this Puerto Rican nigga named Fredo. He's muscular and has geometric patterns tatted on his head. Hard to miss and moves guns on the east side. I could hook you up with a piece if you're interested? No charge."

Caleb felt the warehouse's tall walls beginning to close in on him. He tugged at his collar, hoping it would help him breathe more easily. "Piece?"

"You know what I'm talmbout nigga," he bought his voice down to a whisper, mouth inches away from Caleb's burning ear. "Look, this is Chiraq. A modern-day warzone. I don't know what you're doing without a piece on you. You don't want to get caught lacking. It's dangerous and you don't want to end up like your friend."

Caleb nodded, looking around for Rockit, but he was nowhere to be found. He was confused and emotions bubbled inside of him.

Was this random nigga right? Was he doing his friend a disservice by not sliding?

"I mean your nigga Parks was a real one. He put in work. Can't have him rolling in his grave now, can we?"

Caleb's throat was beginning to close, but he managed to spit out a half-hearted response. "No, but how do you know Parks?"

"I'm affiliated with the G-Ds my nigga. Matter of fact, I'm affiliated with lots of people but that's neither here nor there."

The big-headed man pulled something shiny out of his coat and shoved it in Caleb's hands. It was cold, weighty. Caleb wanted nothing to do with it, but he knew this wasn't a person you said no to.

"Thanks."

"Don't thank me. Just find that nigga Fredo and slide on his muscle head ass. Show him you aren't a coward. Show him your heart. And make good on Parks name. I trust you're capable of doing this. You trust me, right?"

Caleb nodded, shocked by the dream-like interaction. He didn't know what to do. His prints were already on the gun so he shoved it inside his waistband, hoping no one would notice the bulge or question him about it. His eyes darted around the party, scared that something bad was going to happen, that the hardwood underneath him would crack open and swallow him whole.

The big-headed man disappeared into the crowd and Caleb was shook to his core. He closed his eyes and wiped away a tear before it could fully form, looking around for Rockit.

"Hey twin, I ran into Big Poliano."

"*The* Big Poliano? No way. He's got the city going crazy. Heard he just got signed to Pusha T's label."

"Yeah, he invited me to his music video shoot. We're going."

Caleb tried mustering up happiness, but something about this music video shoot felt wrong, but he shoved the feeling away, attributing it to the potent blend of alcohol and pills buzzing around his system like a hornet's nest.

The thought of Parks rolling around his grave and looking down at him in shame stung worse than a thousand executioner wasps.

Diamonds Dancing

Fredo watched Big Poliano bend a girl over with short black hair, gold hoop earrings gleaming under the strobe lights, and a giant peacock tatted on her pear-shaped ass. His heavy chains jingled as she twerked on him. He was surrounded by an entourage of about forty gang members, all ready to ride for him if necessary.

The funny looking nigga with the big head from earlier approached the rapper, asking for an autograph.

"Don't you see I'm busy, my nigga?" Big Poliano grinded on the girl, angrily thrusting his hips forward.

"I'm a big fan though. Just this one time."

Big Poliano smacked the girl's ass and moved her aside. "I'll give you a pic, thirsty ass nigga. How about that?"

"I would love that. Much appreciated, my nigga."

The big-headed nigga draped his arm across Big Poliano's broad back, and cheesed for the cellphone's camera. His grill gleamed like a disco ball in the light.

"Let's get one thing clear, you're a fan. Not my nigga."

"What's understood doesn't have to be stated."

"Get a load of this nigga," Big Poliano said, hitting one of his friend's in the chest, laughing. "We got a comedian on our hands."

"I don't see anyone laughing."

The tension grew thick in the air. *Did this nigga have a death wish?*

"You got a problem, nigga?"

"Only with your fake chains."

"Oh you're a jeweler now? You got some balls on you, nigga. I could put hands on you. Plural." The entourage was moving closer, moving in like a pack of hyenas, ready for the signal to commit violence.

"I never claimed to be a jeweler, but I'm deeply affiliated."

"With who?"

"Many. They are vast, formless, and all-encompassing."

"On folks, what the fuck are you talking about? Motherfucker must be gone off some fentanyl or something."

The big-headed nigga pulled out his diamond tester like a secret weapon, proudly brandishing it in the air. A couple members of Big Poliano's entourage shifted uneasily. A few even tucked their own chains in their coats and shirts, worried about the possibility of being exposed by the technological device.

"I want to see how *real* you are. You willing to take that chance? Are you willing to put that on the line, Big Poliano?"

"I ain't never been scared, nigga. I come from 63rd, the trenches. Let's do it."

The big-headed nigga placed the diamond tester against Big Poliano's exuberant chains. He scanned the diamonds slowly, everyone watched the green bars pop up on the screen, wondering if it would make it into red territory.

The bars stopped right before yellow. Someone gasped.

"Looks like these are fake. I thought you were real? Perhaps I'm mistaken."

Big Poliano's face was sweaty and he looked around the party as if this was some sort of mistake. "You sure that's accurate? How do I know that isn't faulty shit from China?"

"I assure you, it's real unlike you and what you present to the public."

Big Poliano looked as if his ego had taken a blast point-blank from the barrel of a shotgun. He looked back at his crew and his expression turned dark and took on a grim aura.

"Fuck this nigga up."

The entourage swarmed the big-headed nigga, throwing hands until he fell to the ground, disappearing underneath a barrage of Timberland boots coming down on his body. Puncture-resistant rubber soles, 400 grams of Primaloft insulation multiplied by ten, and eco-conscious nubuck leather rained down.

"That's right, stomp that nigga out." Big Poliano commanded. He was beginning to look like himself again.

A random woman screamed, fearful at the display of violence taking place in front of her. One of the gang members paused, pulling out a Draco from the recesses of his large coat, raised it to the sky, and pulled the trigger.

Pop, pop, pop, pop, pop, pop.

More people screamed and figures scurried for every exit leading outside of the warehouse. A man slipped and fell in the midst of the madness and was trampled.

Fredo spotted his client in the crowd with his mustache freaking out and running in the wrong direction, directly toward the cluster of gang members.

"Where are you going, bro?" He yelled, hoping his warning would work.

It was too late. The motherfucker was gone and there was nothing Fredo could do to stop him. He watched Udom bump into the gang member toting the Draco and paused, paralyzed by the offensive slight.

The draco-toting man pointed the gun at Fredo's client and pulled the trigger, blowing a hole in his client's arm. Fredo ran forward, wondering if his luck had gone to complete shit or if this was some strange karma he was paying back to the universe.

His client fell the ground, nursing the bleeding wound in his arm and blood splattered Fredo's kicks.

There's goes eight hundred fuckin dollars down the drain and now my client might die on me. How could this night get any worse?

"Jesus fucking christ, bro."

Police sirens rang in the distance and Fredo's heart sank down to his knees. This was turning out to be a terrible night and he hadn't made a dime off this shit. He wondered why he trusted this guy in the first place? Maybe he should have skipped the party and kept things kosher, but no he felt like going out on a limb for the love of money.

Fredo bent down and kneeled next to his client who was crying, snot running over his mustached lips.

"Text me when you get your life together, bro," Fredo patted him on the head. "Be safe."

Darkness, darkness, darkness, darkness, darkness *congealing*, darkness, darkness, darkness, darkness, darkness, darkness, darkness, darkness, darkness *curdling*, darkness, darkness, darkness, darkness, darkness, darkness, darkness, darkness, darkness, darkness, darkness, darkness, darkness, darkness, darkness, darkness, darkness, darkness *coagulating*,

darkness, darkness, darkness, darkness, darkness
darkness, darkness, darkness, darkness,
darkness *clotting*,
darkness
darkness
darkness
dark...

Fumbling through the darkness, Fredo struggled to find the light switch in his bathroom. He staggered, nearly running into the sink, but he managed to fall to his knees in front of the bathtub. He gripped the shower curtain, vomiting a mess of food chunks and bile.

Fredo drank an entire bottle of tequila after the botched meeting with his client. He tried drinking his troubles away and now he was paying for it in the worst way possible.

He wiped away the snot streaming from his nose and prayed to whatever God that would listen for the vomit to stop. He coughed and his stomach lurched before he bent over again, throwing up a stream of bile. *Jesus Christ, I fucking hate tequila.* Breathing heavily, he wished he would just pass out or die. Anything was better than this small hell.

Another wave of bile came up, and Fredo thought he was reaching the end. The finish line had to be in sight. It fuckin had to. He dry heaved before throwing up more bile, some of it shooting out of his nostrils. Wiping his nose with the edge of his hand, he noticed something small and gleaming floating in the pool of vomit. Well beyond the point of caring about the way he looked, Fredo dug through the throw-up, hating the smell of butyric acid, fishing out the golden object. Feeling drained and emptied, he held the mysterious object up to the light. A hollow point bullet.

How the fuck did this get inside my stomach?

Fredo retched again, dropping the bullet back into the pool of vomit. The tip of the bullet split open like a flower in full bloom. He threw up again, this time coughing up six bullets. Deeply horrified, he thought about calling 911, but he didn't want to bring that type of attention to himself especially considering his particular line of work and his gang affiliation tatted on his body.

Don't put a target on yourself, you dumb fuck.

Growing dizzy, Fredo noticed the room spinning and he passed out on the bathroom floor, dreaming of bullets pouring out of every orifice of his body, ripping through musculature and delicate skin like copper parasites.

"This can't be the end. My brother needs me," he said, biting down on a bullet like candy.

PART TWO
FULL METAL JACKET

Bite the Bullet

Bullet Tooth dragged the tip of his bloodied sword across the face of the soft wet earth in a jagged pattern unbeknownst to man. Arrows whizzed past his oversized head, covered in a black mail coif, music to his cauliflower ears. He carefully stepped over the body of a knight writhing in pain. A vibrant red cross was emblazoned across his metal chest plate. His mouth was still open in the shape of a question mark and a group of buzzards hovered over his strangely shaped tongue drying in the blazing heat.

"What a pity," Bullet Tooth said with an electric hiss. He could smell the stench of infection wading off the knight's intestinal lining. Dysentery would have killed the man in a couple of days even if he didn't have the misfortune of crossing Bullet Tooth's path.

A thick barbed arrow planted in the middle of the knight's sternum stuck out like a sore thumb. Goose feathers flailing in the wind. Four more arrows stuck out of the ground next to the knight.

Bullet Tooth kicked the knight's head as he passed by, enjoying the dead weight of flesh connecting with the tip of his boot.

A cannon boomed in the distance, firing a hollow projectile full of gunpowder. He looked up at the bruised sky, gazing at the ashes from the burning bodies and smiled.

A young knight charged forward, launching a stealthy attack from the cover of dead bodies, letting out a primal roar as he lunged forward at Bullet Tooth with his blade aimed at his neck. Bullet Tooth leaned back on his heels, relishing the close brush with death, the blade singing through air as he inhaled the scent of shit, wet earth, petrichor, and death. It was like a rich slice of decadence. He couldn't get enough. He wanted more. No, he *needed* more, more. Much more.

Much more.

The one hundred and forty second time Bullet Tooth was summoned to this plane of existence was during World War II. A group of Nazis dressed in ceremonial robes performed the Ritual to Mars, thinking a massive sacrifice would bring the God of War to aid them in their campaign. The fools succeeded, but no man could command Bullet Tooth.

He grew fat and obese from the violence, ignoring Adolf's desperate prayers somewhere deep within the earth.

Hitler's thick mustache shimmered with sweat, twitching with fear and his Iron Cross medal looked dull in the dim light of his underground bunker. Cradled by Eva Braun, they inspected two cyanide capsules, dreaming of a better life in

Berchtesgaden, a small town in the Bavarian Alps. They popped the pills with water.

Hitler raised the pistol to his own head, fighting the baleful whispers in his brain and ignoring the shouts coming out of his wretched wife's mouth. There was so much more to do, some much more land to conquer. His index finger squeezed the trigger, ending his reign over Germany.

"Bite your bullets," Bullet Tooth commanded an entire platoon of soldiers. They followed his alluring command, ignoring their instinct for survival, biting down until their teeth cracked or were jammed so deep into their gum line, blood gushed out in waves.

"Good little soldiers," Bullet Tooth chuckled. "Now, our next order of business... bite down on your guns."

A businessman covered in filth and mosquito bites ventured deep into the Aokigahara forest, headed towards the notorious Lake Si Bat Cake with a massive waterproof camping lantern and tattered map in one hand, compass hanging from his wrist, briefcase in the other hand. He left his family without a word after being let go from his corporate job. Something buried deep inside his fractured mind from past generations pulled him deeper into the forest, walking through miles of tightly packed trees, Japanese hemlock, hinoki cypress, conifers, roots winding into eldritch shapes.

Sweat stains bloomed in the armpits of his virgin wool single-breasted blazer. The forest was humid, feeling like a damn sauna. Dabbing his head with a soiled handkerchief, he remembered the brown sign at the entrance that said "Your life is something precious that was given to you by your parents" and spat on the uneven ground. Spit soaked up into the earth, soil rich with magnetic iron, disrupting the compass needle. Smacking the device with the palm of his hand, it righted itself.

What a cruel joke. Thirteen million people in Tokyo and my life is precious? Far from it. Nothing I did for my parents was good enough. No matter how much money I sent them, no matter how many grandchildren I gave them. Nothing I did for my wife and my children was good enough. I'm a disappointment. A sad excuse of a man.

Bullet Tooth could smell the vibrant stench of desperation and depression wading off the businessman like a cheap cologne. Perhaps this would give him the strength he needed to escape his prison. A group of Japanese witches managed to trap him inside the cave with the aid of their ancestors, a binding spell, a series of ancient seals, and a tantalizing piece of bait. He couldn't believe he fell for the trap—a deformed baby of all things. It was a juicy treat, but not enough to give him the extra burst of energy he needed at the time. This wasn't the first time he'd been caught, and he was at peace knowing this wouldn't be the last.

He was well aware of the other spirits, entities, and dark forces inhabiting the forest. Some felt like kindred spirits, dripping with evil, yearning for sad souls to walk down certain trails. He applauded their efforts.

Bullet Tooth was scrawny and weak in his present state, looking like a pair of old tattered clothes pinned to the cave wall, but he knew the businessman would find his way to him. He had laid out a psychic thread, lightly guiding the sad fuck towards him like a fly drawn to a bright light.

The businessman passed by the lava domes, and stepped over the corded lava floor, rippling outward like hardened waves. He hummed a lamentful tune as he moved closer to Bullet Tooth's abode. Ropes swayed in the wind and everything was too quiet, sound swallowed by the dense foliage. He wrapped a red ribbon around a tree, marking a loose trail back to the entrance in case he decided to change his mind and turn back.

A colony of bats flew over the businessman's head, screeching, trying to warn him of the entity's presence within the cave. He was clueless and unable to grasp the language of bats, detached from the spirit world and his own dwindling sense of intuition after spending more than a decade in and out of cold, sterile office spaces.

A single Hilgendorf tube-nosed bat squeaked out in pain as it was devoured by Bullet Tooth. Leathery brown skin discarded like a used condom. The businessman paused for a moment, and continued on, undeterred by the bat's death cry, moving closer to Bullet Tooth's cursed place within the darkness. He carefully unclasped the suitcase and pulled out an ornamental knife and a picture of his family. Smiling faces, harmony, and love flooded from the photo taken two years ago during a family vacation to the coast.

Getting down on his knees, tears spilled out of the businessman's green eyes. He kissed the photo, tenderly caressing the faces of his loved ones before slicing his wrists open and shoving the long knife into his soft belly, jerking it to the left, successfully committing hara-kiri.

Falling forward, he muttered a series of prayers passed down throughout the generations of his cursed bloodline, ultimately calling forth Bullet Tooth.

Bullet Tooth soaked up the blood, gaining new life and stepped down on the ground for the first time in ages. He went on a rampage for decades before being caught by a trio of shamans, bounding him to his own realm long before Caleb called his name.

Resting Gun Face

"Is that Rihanna or Jasmine? Bitch, I can't tell the difference."

Jasmine sat on a fake concrete block, leaning her weight on her left arm, right arm hidden behind her. She stared into the camera, and mouthed thank you. Easing into the relaxed pose, she pictured olive trees surrounding her and warm air blowing through her hair.

Click.

Jasmine's petite body was decked out in a Nurul cream-colored handwoven set made in a third-generation artisan workshop in Gaza. A boxy cropped top and an a-line maxi skirt with elasticated waists. Vibrant pink, green, and orange stripes ran down the middle of the Majdalawi fabric broken only by her exposed tan stomach. Sahar hoop earrings dangled from her ears, a gold-plated pendant featuring an evil eye encompassed by the sun and moon.

The intersectional fashion brand was called nöl collective formerly known as Babyfist, probably her favorite clothing designer of all time. Sustainable Palestinian clothing brimming with ancestral and indigenous knowledge. Wearing these pieces made her feel whole, made her feel rooted in her homeland, and connected to her people.

"Outfit change," Jasmine said, skipping into the portable changing room and pulling the curtain closed. "Be out in ten, Rodrigo."

"Take your time, sis."

Jasmine took off her clothes and carefully folded them on the bench. Goosebumps formed on her arms as she squeezed into a midnight blue teddy with scalloped lace trim and velvet bows. She dug into her duffle bag and pulled out some deodorant, applied it, and spritzed herself with some perfume. Inhaling the pleasant floral scent, she felt like an angel.

"I'm ready for the spotlight," Jasmine said, spinning in a dramatic circle and bowed elegantly.

"You're serving absolute cunt," Rodrigo said, getting into position with his camera.

"I knew it," Jasmine said, moving into her first pose.

The blue-haired photographer bent down, adjusting his transparent ORTUU Augustus top with subtle floral details and raglan sleeves. His green Chester pants swept the ground as he took a knee, changing the camera's aperture, and framed Jasmine asymmetrically in the camera's viewfinder. She tilted her chin demurely while a sustainable mink coat hung loosely off her shoulders with two FN F2000 machine guns in each hand. Small green veins popped out of her triceps as she held the weapons upright, waiting for the click of the camera. She turned away from the camera with a fierce look in her eyes.

"You look snatched, bitch," the photographer said.

"Rodrigo, you're magical."

"Am I?" He said, snapping a few more shots.

"Shut up, you know I don't compliment people like that. If I said it, I meant it."

"You're too sweet," he got down on the floor, belly-first, to get a new angle. "Give me divine feminine. Give me high priestess."

Jasmine turned to the side and waited for the shutter to click. Then she laid down in a seductive pose, mouth slightly agape.

"Yasssssssss, that's exactly what I need."

"Thanks."

"Hold on, I have an idea. You'll love it."

Rodrigo dug through a trunk of random objects and pulled out a rug. It was an authentic Canadian polar bear fur rug and it was much more massive than it looked once it was unfurled on the background paper hanging in the studio and covering a portion of the floor.

"That looks amazing."

"I know, right? I want you to lie down on this polar bear with your fine ass and do what you do best with those ridiculous guns."

"You mean shoot?"

"No, bitch. I don't need the cops breaking down the doors."

"I could take out a precinct with these guns."

"That's cool and all, but don't point these guns in my direction. I'm too fine to die at my age and I have so much more I plan on accomplishing."

Jasmine softened her tone. "Rodrigo, I'm not going to take my photographer out. No one can do what you do. Seriously a lot of these photographers suck and cis men just want to fuck me on set. You're one of one. I meant that."

"Aww thanks babe. I know they're posers and pervs."

Jasmine laid down on her stomach and propped her elbows on the polar bear's furry back, raising her guns skyward. It was surprisingly comfortable.

"Does my ass look fat?" She tried to look back at her ass popping out of her blue thong.

"It's small, but it's a fatty. And I'll make sure it pops with the angles. Don't you worry, I got you."

"Awww thanks. That makes me feel a lot better."

"Girl, I wish I was snatched like you." He patted his small gut hidden beneath his white shirt.

"Shut up."

Trying out a few different facial expressions, Jasmine feigned innocence, a coy demeanor, an angry snarl, followed by a sensual glare directed at the camera's lens.

"Oh hold that expression. It's giving resting gun face."

Jasmine started into the eye of the camera, exuding confidence, and dripping sexiness.

Rodrigo fanned himself with his free hand. "Oh you might fuck around and make me straight girl."

"You're going to make me blush."

"What are you doing this weekend? Got big plans?"

"I'm supposed to be in Big Poliano's music video this weekend."

"Shut the fuck up."

"I swear to Allah it's going down. I met him at an underground party. It was crazy. Some poor guy got stomped out and someone started shooting the place up."

"Oh shit, are you okay? Obviously, you didn't get hurt, but that's too much for me. I would have been gone in a jiffy."

"I'm good. Me and the girls managed to get out of there pretty quick."

Rodrigo placed his hand on his heart. "Well that's a relief."

"Sure is."

"Now back to my man, Big Poliano. He's sexy A-F."

"He's overrated in real life. Plus, he's sexist and smells like a bag of weed. And get this — he said feminism is quote 'exhausting.'"

"Why are you doing it then? I know he objectifies women and talks down on them. I don't see the appeal outside of getting some celebrity D."

"Don't just cross a river, cross it bearing fire."

"That just gave me chills, bitch, but I need some elaboration."

"It's complicated, Rodrigo. I'm mainly doing it for exposure, but if someone looks me up after seeing me shake my ass in the video, they'll learn something about feminism or maybe even what's going on in Palestine. I'm thinking bigger picture. Sometimes we gotta make these sacrifices."

"Hey you never know, right?" Rodrigo shrugged.

"Exactly. Can you put on some music?"

Rodrigo pulled out his phone and scrolled through some songs and hit play. Ice Spice's "In Ha Mood" blared through the speakers.

"This is my shit. What you know about my baby Ice?"

"Bitch, don't you know who I am? I stay in the know."

Jasmine bopped to the song, swinging her small hips back and forth to the beat, and stuck her tongue out. Her mind drifted back to see the video shoot and she wondered what she should wear. An outfit was everything and she wanted to make a statement that no one would forget.

Flash.

Exit Stage Left

The bootleg man cracked open a beer with his teeth, taking great pride in the condition of his pearly whites. His ex-wife encouraged him to give up alcohol years ago, he clearly remembered the worry painted on her face but paid the nagging no mind. There was a certain satisfaction he gained by opening the alcohol in such a savage fashion. Made him feel like a real man, made the reptilian part of his brain light up like a supernova, and most importantly made him feel good.

He slumped down onto the couch, took a long sip, and gazed at the towers of VHS tapes and stacks of bootlegged DVDs and Blu-rays teetering on the brink of collapse. It was a diverse collection and he always wondered who would inherit this treasure trove after his death. His mortality hovered around him like a poltergeist, and he wanted someone to appreciate these the way he had.

He hated the constant advances in technology, wishing time could come to a standstill. It made him feel like an archaeological artifact holding onto a distant past, quickly dissolving.

Downing the rest of the beer, he wondered if his services were no longer needed. He used to feel like a pillar of the community, the last sentry protecting the forces of cinema.

Was that a convenient lie, Devin? You're nothing more than a delusional old man. I mean you have to force people to buy shit from you week after week. And don't get me started on the annoyance in people's eyes, the hate and irritation in their body language...but you choose to ignore it like a fool. What's the point? Maybe you should off yourself...

Devin shook his head, forcing the onslaught of negative thoughts down into a dark pit. Still, they wriggled around his head like a pinball, banging around his subconscious with a frightening speed.

"Time for some liquid sustenance," he said aloud, opening the fridge. The soft light buzzed and glitched, dying out completely. He thought about calling maintenance but figured it was too late in the day for them to make a visit.

He grabbed another beer, ready to escape through the alcohol, and sauntered over to his massive movie collection. Closing his eyes, he grabbed a random VHS tape and gently pushed it into the slot of his dual DVD/VHS tape player.

The screen popped and fizzled and *Candyman* was displayed on the screen in prominent white letters. He was happy he owned the original and not the sequel. Taking another sip, he remembered walking past a newly-built theater playing the flick, and he vehemently refused to waste a single cent. CGI ruined movies and these half-brained people posing as directors had no idea what they were doing in this time and age.

A tear ran down his eye as he watched the screen jump a few scenes. He could hear the tape whirring, showing signs of age and wear, struggling to play properly. Another tear streamed down his cheek as he remembered playing in the Cabrini Green projects as a teenager, and he sniffled.

Older folks referred to it as "Little Hell" thanks to the constant gang wars raging rampant throughout the housing projects. He remembered the ferocity of the Egyptian Cobras and the Black Deuces before they were swallowed up by the Black Disciples, and then the steady influx of Vice Lords moving in. Nothing but violence, crime, and gunshots spread throughout the neighborhood like an invisible plague.

The screen filled with the image of Candyman opening his crusty mouth, pulling the blond graduate student Helen Lyle in close. A swarm of bees poured from his mouth and crawled on his brown cheeks. A soft murmuration. Ominous music played in the background and the buzzing grew louder, amplified by the sharp scream of Helen piercing through his speakers. His ears rang and his head swam as Devin struggled to turn the volume down just so he could think straight.

Feeling like a character inside a dream, Devin ventured into his bedroom, bent down, and fished around for the Nike shoebox underneath his bed. They used to house his original 1972 Bruin basketball shoes with the blue swoosh on the side until the sole started falling apart and he tossed them out. He pulled the box out, feeling a sense of overwhelming relief.

Going back into the living room, he set it down on the table and stared at it while *Candyman* continued playing on the television. He went into the kitchen and grabbed two more beers.

His movements were becoming more sluggish. He couldn't drink the way he used to. Doctor said it was fucking up his liver, but he didn't care. He knew his biological clock was ticking and he was going to enjoy himself while he still had time.

What is there left to enjoy, oldhead? No one cares about your bootleg tapes and fucked up DVDs. Give it up already. You're about as useful as those old shoes you threw out last Christmas.

The bootleg man was surprised by the steady downpour of tears coming down his face. *What did people call this again? Oh yeah, the dark night of the soul.* He was going through it and then some.

He took the top off the shoebox and tossed it aside, revealing a Taurus 856 .38 Special Revolver he purchased a decade ago for protection. The gangs were going crazy these days, shooting each other when it got too hot out and he felt himself slowing down with age. He never considered committing suicide with this revolver, but the idea was becoming more and more attractive.

Feeling the cold weight of the gun in his hands, he wondered if anyone would miss him. He never fathered any children, a sticky knot of regret swimming around his stomach. No one checked on him outside of few older folk and a couple church ladies.

No one feels sorry for you, old man. Just end it.

Something knocked on the living room window and it broke Devin out of his suicidal reverie.

"Who the fuck?"

He got up to investigate the disturbance and moved towards the window with his revolver in hand. Slowly approaching the window, the buzzing of bees somehow grew louder. Pulling the coned strings, the blinds rose, cheap plastic accordioning upwards, revealing a night sky. He shoved the window upwards, feeling the harsh wind cut his face. No animals moved outside, and he was five stories up so it made no sense that a person would be able to climb this high, especially in the dead of winter.

He closed the window and heard something clatter in the living room and a tower of DVDs tumbled downward. Turning around, he found a .33 Nosler bullet rolling back and forth on the floor until it came to a complete standstill.

Something about it unsettled him at his core. He didn't remember touching a bullet earlier, but he was tipsy and he had a bad case of cottonmouth. He could have easily forgotten pulling out the case of bullets, but the ammo was too big for his gun.

Sitting down on the couch, he looked up, waiting for some form of divine intervention to happen. After about twenty minutes passed, he decided it was time.

Do it, you old useless piece of shit. Do yourself and the world a favor and get it over with. You're only taking up space at this point.

Devin sobbed, snot running over his trembling lips. With a shaky hand, he raised the loaded gun to his temple, fighting the need for self-preservation pounding through his basal ganglia. He ran his tongue over the roof of his mouth and the room seemed to close in on him. A fisheye lens view barricaded by a flood of suicidal thoughts.

Get it together and don't fuck this up. You don't want to become a paralyzed mess living out the rest of your days in a hospital eating slop and taking pills. Do it and do it well.

He gritted his teeth, waiting for his hands to stop shaking and pulled the trigger, blowing his brains out. As the last vestiges of consciousness seeped out of his body, he heard a burst of electrical laughter filling every inch of the living room with a malicious tenor, overshadowing the horror flick playing on TV.

Bullet Tooth stood outside in the cold with prominent purple bruises on his face, feeding off the violence that just took place. He snorted the potent energy like a line of coke, breathing life into his skinny frame. His stomach grew fatter, and he rubbed his gut, thoroughly satisfied from the smorgasbord of pain and misery in the air.

Therapy Session #2

Caleb played around with his tangled headphones, fascinated by the white knots. He had no idea how the cords became so intricately knotted inside his pockets. Usually he wore airpods, but they died on the walk over and he wanted to be prepared for the walk home.

"Give me a second to find a pen that works," his therapist said. This was the first time Caleb ever saw her flustered and out of control. She whipped out drawer after drawer, frantically searching for a proper writing utensil.

"No worries. Take your time."

Caleb blew a piece of lint off his headphones before wedging his thumbnail into a loose opening, penetrating the tight space. Pinching a part of the cord in between his thumb and index finger, he pulled away, freeing up a new portion of the cords. Satisfied with his handiwork, he got to work on another tightly bound knot while his therapist began calming down since she found a pen that actually worked.

"Okay finally found one." She sat down, pushed a few strands of hair behind her ears, adjusted her shirt collar and smoothed out a wrinkle on her skirt. "Sorry for the chaos. I'll make sure you get a full session."

"No worries. I was solving my own problem over here." He held up his tangled headphones, proudly dangling them in the air.

His therapist nodded, unconcerned with the headphones. "Look Caleb, I'm going to be frank... I'm concerned about you. You look like you lost weight and your eyes..."

"What's wrong with my eyes?" Caleb asked, rubbing them with his knuckles, knowing the dark circles were a glaring reflection of his emotional state.

"You look exhausted. Are you getting enough sleep? Did something happen since our last session? Are you dreaming about Parks again?"

Caleb slouched down in his chair and his lower back ached. He looked around the room and picked at the black dirt underneath his fingernails.

"No, not really."

There goes another lie released into the wild like a bird. You just can't help yourself, can you?

"I think I'm getting a decent amount of sleep. I'm having a bit of paranoia though."

"What type of paranoia? Could you elaborate?"

"I guess you could call it paranoia surrounding a demon. A boogeyman of sorts. Let's say one of your demons got loose and you need to get rid of it, theoretically, what would you do?"

The therapist adjusted her glasses, thinking this scenario over. "I would kill it, get rid of the thing or figure out a way to stop the habits feeding the demon."

Caleb nodded. "But what if this is a really big demon? An intimidating demon?" Caleb hunched over, clasping his hands. "Something that could *hurt* you and everyone you love."

"I'd be scared, but I would try to research this demon, educate myself so I know how to tackle it in the future."

"That's not a bad idea," Caleb said, thinking it over. "Research."

"Caleb, is this demon talk code for something else like depression, suppressed emotions or are you deflecting from the question at hand?"

Caleb ran his hands through his dreads, feeling the ridges of each loc. "...yeah...sure."

"I thought so. Make sure you're getting enough sleep and eating regularly. You need to fulfill your basic needs to reduce the severity of your depression. Give it a month and I promise you'll start feeling better."

"I got you."

"Did you bring those drawings in like I asked?"

"Oh yeah, almost forgot." Caleb dug inside his backpack and pulled out a thick spiral-bound sketchbook and handed it over to his therapist.

The therapist licked her thumb and index finger, flipping open the sketchbook. It revealed a number of expressive charcoal drawings. Thick strokes, moody shadows, and the heavy weight of the pencil were evident in the lines outlining the figures.

The first drawing was a zombie dinosaur with rotting flesh, exposed musculature, and bones sticking out of its ribcage. A pool of black tar and heavy vegetation served as the landscape. Looming shadows with sharp cross-hatching bled off into the negative space. The next page depicted a fetus surrounded by bullets in a rough spiral. There was a distinct sense of anguish and pain emanating from the unborn offspring. The following page displayed an oversized head with cauliflower ears, a blue tongue laid out in an erotic fashion, tastebuds protruding like a sea of erections, and a cartoonishly large grin, sporting bullets in the place of teeth, shimmering like stars in the night despite being black and white.

The therapist's delicate left hand trembled as she attempted to adjust her glasses which fell off her face, clattering on her oak desk.

"Are you okay?" Caleb asked, genuinely worried. He had never seen his therapist shaken before, let alone distressed

"Y-yes," she bent over picking up her glasses. "I was just taking in the *enormity* of these drawings. There's a profound darkness and emotional vibrance present."

"Well what do you think of my art?" Caleb rubbed his hands together.

"To be honest, Caleb, I'm taken aback. Astonished, really."

"Thanks."

"They're provocative and show a great deal of emotion and I've barely scratched the psychological surface of this sketchbook."

"Is this the part where you give me a deep psychoanalysis?"

"Not exactly, but why is the subject matter so dark? So bleak? So uncompromising? There's not a single shred of hope in any of your drawings."

"That's my perspective, my view of the world. That's Chicago. That's the hood, that's my truth."

The therapist took down some notes and then looked up at Caleb speechless.

"It's my outlet," Caleb continued, trying his best to reassure her. He didn't want to be put in the crazy house. He had more than enough to worry about as it is. "Helps me purge the demons."

"That's great, Caleb," she said, forcing a smile. "You have a lot of talent. Have you considered trying to place your art in a show or a gallery?"

"I haven't given it serious thought, but I'm playing around with the idea of putting in the school art show. First place gets two years of college tuition paid for."

"That's amazing. You should do it. It's good to be recognized for your talents. Maybe you should have a couple of lighter pieces to go with the dark ones. You know, to balance it out."

Caleb nervously laughed, pulling at the headphones sitting in his lap. "That's not a bad idea. I'll think about it."

"Great."

"Great."

Caleb took his sketchbook and shoved it back into his bag, feeling vulnerable despite the positive praise he received from his therapist. He threw his hood back over his head and awkwardly said bye. Leaving the office, he had a hard time shaking the image of his therapist's eyes when she looked at his drawings and the sense of alarm in her movements.

She was shook.

Rubbing his hands furiously together, Caleb tried to get some heat going into his cold body.

"It's fucking cold in here Miss Kerrigan," one of his classmates exclaimed.

"Trevor, watch your language," Miss Kerrigan took a sip of her peppermint hot chocolate.

"The heater is broken, and we all have to deal with it. The school has maintenance coming by to fix it. So god willing it'll be fixed by tomorrow."

Miss Kerrigan was bundled up in a green oversized coat, zipped to the apex, and her face was paler than usual, cheeks rosy red. She looked like she was suffering just as much as the rest of the class.

Caleb's hands were growing numb despite blowing into them. Still, he typed on his computer, trying his best to ignore the physical pain, searching for a solution to the monstrosity known as Bullet Tooth.

He learned about the bootleg man's death when he stumbled on a physical copy of the local newspaper *The Chicago Tribune* at the barbershop. It was a small write-up on the bootlegger that spoke about his life and how he was found dead inside his apartment after committing suicide. It made no sense why he would kill himself. Caleb knew it was no coincidence and it had to be Bullet Tooth's doing.

Nothing came up when he directly looked up Bullet Tooth in the search engines, frustrating Caleb to no end. He wondered if Bullet Tooth was a nickname and maybe he had to search deeper pockets of the web. He skimmed through faded PDFs of grimoires, occult texts, and eventually stumbled on something that piqued his interest inside a strange digital book called the Necronomicon.

About three-quarters into the book, there was a small section on an entity called Dente Labe Bulla. It had an oversized head resembling Bullet Tooth's, but the body was skinnier, scrunched up into a fetal position floating in something similar to egg yolk and mucus. The webpage glitched, causing the image to stretch out in cascading waves of black, filling the screen in erratic patterns of darkness.

Click, click, click, click.

Sweat ran down the base of Caleb's neck, surprising him and bringing him back down to earth. He clicked the circular refresh symbol over and over until it finally gave way, and the page returned to normal. This had to be Bullet Tooth, the similarities were uncanny and the energy dripping off the drawing was malicious and violent. There was a small description of the entity being dangerous and parallel dimensions. However, there was no advice on how to kill it or get rid of it in totality.

"Caleb, you seem engrossed. What exactly are you working on?" Miss Kerrigan asked as she slowly moved around the computer to look at his monitor.

Caleb hurried and clicked on a different tab showcasing expressive artwork by Chris Bachalo, David Mack, Mike Mignola, and Jean Michael Basquiat. He prayed that his teacher would ignore the other tabs.

Miss Kerrigan hunched over the table, looking at Bachalo's artwork, admiring the penwork and line density. Caleb caught a whiff of her lavender scent, unsure if it was deodorant or perfume. He liked it though, contemplating if he should compliment her or not.

"You have some solid inspiration here. I need to look into this Bachalo guy more deeply. I can see subtle hints of his work in your drawings. Keep it up."

"Thanks."

Relieved, Caleb discreetly watched his teacher sit back down behind her desk before he clicked back on the important tab. He scrolled through a few other pages highlighting a rolodex of deities and demons but couldn't find a simple solution to the motherfucker known as Bullet Tooth.

How did people figure out this shit back in the day? There was no Internet and you had to travel to libraries. And who's to say you would find the right book? Am I going to die before 21? Is this something I need to accept? I always thought I'd overdose on pills or commit suicide. Never considered dying by the hands of a thing called Bullet Tooth or Bulla. And what kind of name is Bulla? Sounds like a goofy ass nigga.

An invisible weight crawled on Caleb's back and his chest grew heavy at the thought of death encroaching. He was swimming in depression, but his art always gave him a sense of hope, a potential way out from the weight of his negative thoughts, an escape route from the bullshit in Chicago. It was hard enough dealing with paranoia and the ever-present danger looming in the streets. Now, he somehow unleashed an entity onto the world and he felt responsible for the bootleg man's death. He had to fix things before Bullet Tooth caused more unnecessary bloodshed.

Death had never been this palpable, never this up close and personal. Caleb wished he had a perc or something to eradicate these heavy feelings and disconnect from it all. Time was ticking and he had to figure something out before things spiraled out of control.

Guns R Us

Fredo slowly turned into the Graceland Cemetery, drove around until he found the right spot, parked, and got out of the car. He stuffed his hands into his pockets, searching for warmth. His shoes crunched on the snow as he made his way towards the grave.

"Here we are."

Fredo fished his phone out his coat pocket and hit record. With his free hand, he pulled his dick out and pissed on the gravestone, hot steam rising in the air. He made sure he doused the name Jamar Parks in yellow. Then he moved the thick stream downward, hitting the bouquet of flowers, drowning the petals in piss.

He shook his dick out before tucking it back into his boxers. Turning the screen view back on himself, he smiled directly into the camera.

"Hope you rest in piss, fuck nigga."

"This is impressive," Udom said, slowly moving around the room in awe with a cast on his left arm, signatures covering the fiberglass like graffiti. He studied the full gamut of guns on display in the Air bnb with the reverence of a rare art collector.

There was a SIG MPX-K 9mm mounted on the wall next to a Mossberg 590 Shotgun, a Magnum Research Desert Eagle, a Sig Sauer P320 AXG Equinox, a Zastava ZPAP M70, a Century Arm Draco Nak9, a Mossberg 590 Shockwave, a FN Scar 20S, a .50 Bewoulf, a JTS M12 AR, along with a diverse assortment of guns on every single table. Udom's gaze moved away from the guns and looked into the black eye of a home camera staring down with a blinking blue light, recording every aspect of the transaction taking place.

"Thanks bro, I take a lot of pride in my work," Fredo said.

"I feel like a kid in a candy store. There are so many guns here, it's simply breathtaking," Udom caressed the barrel of a Mossberg like a long-lost lover. "How long did it take you to set this up? Do you have help? You have to have help. It's so elaborate."

"You got a lot of questions, bro," Fredo side-eyed him, but pushed his paranoia aside. Something about this nigga screamed money and deep pockets despite his annoying ass questions. "Well I'll let you in on a trade secret, no man is ever truly alone in this world, especially when they're part of a nation."

"Oh you're referring to People's Nation, specifically Vice Lords?"

"Damn, we got a certified genius in the room." Fredo clapped his hands. "Look at that shit."

Udom nervously smiled and turned his attention back to the gun display.

"What are you thinking about buying? I saw you eyeing the Mossberg."

"It's beautiful. I might purchase that or the Desert Eagle."

"You're annoying as fuck, but you have fantastic taste in guns, bro."

"I'm your bro?" Udom's eyes lit up. "I didn't know we were cool like that. I mean we did hang out at the club before the unfortunate circumstances happened."

"Naw, let's get something straight, you're a client and I'm the seller. That's it. Nothing more. Bro is just an expression I use for everyone. Am I clear?"

"Yeah, super clear."

"Good. If you can't make up your mind, we can do a two-for-one special?"

"You know me too well. I'll do it." Udom settled on the Desert Eagle and the Mossberg, and handed Fredo a leather bag full of money.

Fredo took the stacks of money out one by one and ran them through his electronic money counter, making sure the agreed-upon amount was all there.

"We're good?" Udom asked, dragging two gun cases with his healthy arm.

"We're gucci. Nice doing business with you and I appreciate the extra money you put in there for the damaged kicks."

"Of course. I really felt bad about what happened at the club, especially since I invited you out. Big Poliano's a wild one."

"Yeah, it's all good."

"You know what? Speaking of social events, there's a music video shoot he's filming this weekend over on the Low End. You should come. I'm sure you could get more clients over there."

"Damn, that's not a bad idea," Fredo could already hear the sound of the money counter, softly counting stacks in a manner of seconds. "I wish I had a referral program or something. You'd be getting discounts left and right."

"I don't require that, but I appreciate the thought. I'll text you the address."

Udom started heading toward the door, but stopped and turned around.

"Hold on, I almost forgot something," Udom said, digging into his right pocket. He pulled out a small rectangular glass box. "I have a gift for you, from the gods."

"You already paid. I don't need a gift or anything like that. I appreciate you, but—"

"No, I implore you to take this. I was compelled to give this to you and it's quite special. You should at least take a look."

Fredo took the box in hand, confused by the gesture. Sometimes women would offer head or people would tip him in cash, but he never received a physical gift. He was somewhat touched.

"Lemme see..." Fredo observed the glass box in hand, which contained something that looked like a mummified finger wrapped in green thread. There were flecks of gold and fragmented pieces of black obsidian and amethyst surrounding the finger. A strange sensation ran up his arm as he held the box like a zap of energy.

"What the hell is this bro?"

"It's a child's finger from Thailand."

"What the fuck bro? I'm not into organ trafficking or weird shit."

"Take a breath. I don't deal in organ trafficking or anything of the sort. This is a talisman imbued with magical properties. It was meant for you at this specific time."

"I don't practice magic though. What am I supposed to do with this?" Fredo grew hot and nauseous. "This doesn't make any sense to me, bro. C'mon, make it make sense."

"This talisman will bring you protection and good luck. This is something you could use in your line of work and there's nothing you have to do. However, if you wish to amplify the magical properties inside, you need to offer merit on occasion."

"Merit?"

"Offerings to the ghost of the child. Like a bowl of rice, whiskey or good deeds."

"Ghosts can get drunk off whiskey?"

"They can do a lot of things. Western society doesn't teach you the old ways. It's sad, really."

"Hold up, why didn't this shit protect you at the club?"

"I left my protective talisman in the car. It slid out of my coat pocket into the driver's seat. A rare occurrence, I assure you."

"Damn, betchu you won't get caught lackin again without your talisman, huh?"

"You already know. That was a painful lesson from the universe, but I accept it in kind."

"Well, thanks... I guess. Do you have fingers and shit at your crib?"

"I have a wide variety of talismans and guns. I'm a collector of sorts. I too own a finger, but every talisman serves a unique purpose."

"Bet."

They shook hands and Fredo watched Udom leave the Air bnb. He thought about helping ole boy with his guns, but didn't feel like wasting the energy or even asking the question. He felt better now that he had an uptick in his cash-flow and he was thankful that he did good business above all else.

Smelling the stacks of money made him beam and he loved the idea of potentially making more bands off the gang members who would show up at Big Poliano's video shoot. He had a good feeling about this shoot and what might come out of it.

He ran the currency through the money counter again. The beeping sound was like music to his ears. Things were starting to look up for once and Fredo wondered how long this streak would last.

Pole Talk

Jasmine tried on ten different outfits in preparation for the video shoot and took her sweet time doing her makeup. She wanted to look perfect. She had no idea what could come out of this, but she felt like something special might happen.

After trying on multiple outfits, she settled on a white tee that depicted two doves carrying a ribbon over a heart that said "not your habibti" encircled in a ring of blue flowers. She took the excess fabric at the bottom of her shirt and stretched it behind her back, tying it into a tight knot. It gave her boobs an extra umph and exposed her flat stomach. She settled on a pair of green Syrian pants with maroon and tan stripes running down the thigh. Made by three brothers in an Askar refugee camp on the outskirts of Nablus, who she was sure would be pleased to see the way the cotton/polyester blend hugged her hips. She grabbed her ultra-luxe faux sherpa utility gear jacket and her sparkling pink VVS diamond chain in the shape of a Glock.

"Damn, bitch, you're serving face," she said while staring at herself in the mirror.

Lacing up her black Prada Monolith combat boots, she looked up at her reflection, noticing a subtle change in her features. Underneath the soft radiant skin, underneath the layers of makeup, something dark and churning struggled to surface. A flash of her gun, the man crumbling to the ground like papier mache, the walls closing in on her. She shuddered as something monstrous gleamed in the mirror.

Shaking off the image, Jasmine snapped a couple of selfies, did some quick edits, and posted them on social media with the caption "Face card valid." She hoped they looked as good as she thought they did.

Jasmine took a shot of Henny to get rid of any nerves and put her in a better headspace. She ran down two flights of stairs leading to the parking garage, alcohol warming her chest. Her steps resounded throughout the concrete space and the lights flickered. She hopped in her car, thankful to be inside the safe shell of aluminum, plastic, iron ore, glass, and rubber.

A dormant memory rose to the surface as her left hand tightened around the steering wheel. Snatched back to the orphanage, a much younger Jasmine under blankets, adjusted her book reading light, hoping the brightness wouldn't alert the staff to her late night activities. She clutched a brown Barbie stuffed in the crook of her small arm. The black hair was displaced and a few fingers were missing, deep grooves from former owners scratched into its plastic face. Scars that reminded Jasmine of her own, not physical, but emotional tissue damaged by the passage of time and the lack of warmth from her parents. Still, her Barbie gave her comfort, a resilient friend that tried to keep her heart from freezing over.

Miss you, she thought, struggling to remember what happened to her Barbie and how her friend's life came to an end. Jasmine sniffled, realizing that her eyes were wet. She pulled a tissue out of the glove compartment and dabbed her eyes, making sure her makeup wasn't messed up. Taking a breath, she pushed a button and the engine roared to life. The heated seat warmed her bottom, easing her anxiety and longing for the past.

She slowly typed the address into Google Maps, squeezing the life out of her phone, and pulled off.

Something about this part of the city felt darker and untethered from the other blocks, the colors muted and washed out. The street numbers dropped as Jasmine approached the infamous part of Chicago commonly referred to as the Low End. The numbers felt like a celestial timer, constructed by Iblis, counting down to something tenebrous, and bombastic.

The buildings seemed to have layers of decay and grime underneath the frost coating the exteriors, eating into the brick, seeping into the foundation. Bare trees loomed overhead, gnarled limbs shaking in the wind. Sugar maple she recalled. The words tasted tart and acidic in her mouth. Sugar maple. Rounded sinuses, and pointed tips were the distinguishing characteristics.

She heard parts of Bronzeville were getting bought out and redeveloped, but those were only sections. Sections that were nowhere in sight. Big Poliano grew up in this area, specifically shouting out Welch World on multiple songs. She wondered which block belonged to the rapper, which vacant lot gave birth to the violent rhythms, anger, and wordplay that percolated inside his overweight body.

Cop cars had a street blocked off, so Jasmine assumed she made it to the right place. She halfway expected something more luxurious like a mini-mansion and an assortment of fancy cars sprawled in the driveway, but this was some hood shit.

The apartment complexes lining the street were in terrible condition and the few "homes" resembled ruins with plywood covering the windows and charred porches jutting forward. She knew she was out of her element and wondered if she should take her ass back home.

You're overreacting Jas, it's just a video shoot. Nothing crazy's going to happen especially with cops being out here. Calm your paranoid ass down.

Jasmine brought her Glock as a safety measure, shoving it into the interior of her jacket. No one would notice and she had to have her baby on her. Something about this place gave her the creeps.

She got out the car and headed down the block, hearing Big Poliano's music blasting out of a set of speakers. Two drones flew overhead capturing shots of the hood. Portable lights were strategically placed around the street, illuminating the rapper and his crew.

A sense of relief washed over her when she saw the rapper with his massive entourage. Everyone toted large guns, waving them around nonchalantly. Two men directed the crowd, commanding people to move like chess pieces and cameras were shifted into key positions.

"This shit's official," Jasmine said, genuinely impressed by the video shoot and the crew running things.

A few men smoked blunts while a few scantily clad women shook their asses despite the freezing temperature. She wondered if they cared about getting sick or just didn't give a fuck.

Maybe being in your favorite rapper's video was worth the possibility of catching pneumonia? Some people are just wired differently.

"Jasmine, you made it." Big Poliano came over, eyes hidden behind Gucci shades, and gave her a tight hug.

"Of course, I'm a woman of my word."

"I fuck with that. That's why you're my gun-toting nigga."

Jasmine pulled out her Glock, brandishing it proudly. "You know I had to bring my baby with me."

"That's what's up. I remember seeing that shit online. It's nice."

"Thanks."

"Make yourself comfortable. There aren't any rules or anything like that. All these guns are real. Authentic. I'm not fucking with any props. This is real street shit. Ain't nuthin fake out here."

"I feel you."

"These glasses were made in Italy. Crafted from sage acetate," he said, lowering them an inch so she could see his brown eyes. "Foreign shit."

Who gives a shit? And why is he trying to flex? Gucci's an Italian fashion brand, dumbass. God, I hate men.

"Cool."

Big Poliano shifted from side to side, obviously not wanting to leave. He stared at her chest and Jasmine felt uncomfortable.

"What's habibti mean?" he asked. "Peruvian or something like that right?"

Jasmine scoffed. "It's Arabic, means my beloved, my love or my baby depending on the context."

"Oh my bad," he scratched his neck and looked around. "Well help yourself to a drink and do whatever."

Jasmine walked over to a plastic table full of alcohol, trays of food, and baggies of colorful pills. She poured herself a liberal shot of Henny and took it to the head. She was ready to loosen up and have a good time.

"Go ahead," one of the directors yelled. Someone in a fitted cap lit a match and tossed it into two strategically placed cop cars. A brilliant purple flame erupted from the interior, whooshing into the sky. It was an ethereal sight that was both beautiful and nerve-racking.

The directors filmed Big Poliano empathically rapping along to his viral song "Pole Talk pt. 4" as the purple fire raged in the background. The night air was charged with a tense energy that made Jasmine uneasy. She shoved the feeling aside as she bopped along to the song as the men pointed guns at the camera menacingly.

She went back for another shot and saw a familiar face in the crowd. Her heart sank as she did a double-take and saw the light-skinned nigga from the gun range, smoking a fat blunt and carrying heat. He sported an obnoxious bandage covering the gash she inflicted last week.

Don't fucking tell me...This shit's gotta be some sort of joke or something because what's the odds he would be here of all places? Allah, you better have my back.

Jasmine panicked, unsure if she should hide in the crowd or discreetly leave the shoot and run back to her car. She felt trapped and didn't know what the fuck to do. Pouring herself two shots, she took a deep breath and downed one.

"Hey Jasmine, what are you doing here?" Fredo said.

She hugged him, relieved by his presence. "I-I was invited by Big Poliano. Thought it was a good opportunity."

"Nice. Are you okay? You seem shaken up."

"I'm good, just cold. Should have worn more layers under my sherpa."

"Ah, okay... I got something for you, but promise me you won't freak out."

"Oh really?"

"Yeah, but promise me first."

Jasmine put her pinky finger out and Fredo curled his pinky around hers.

"Pinky promise."

Fredo pulled the talisman out of his pocket and handed it over. "It's a protective piece. I thought you might like it even though it's weird as hell."

Jasmine looked at the finger in awe, spinning it in circles. She liked the gold and amethyst even though it was morbid. "Does this really work?"

"Yeah, why not?"

"Didn't peg you as a nigga who dabbled in magic."

Fredo shrugged. "I have different sides to me. Plus, this felt right, you know?"

"Thank you. This means a lot. You have no fuckin idea."

"You're welcome."

"Well I have to go network and get this money. Maybe we can grab a drink after the shoot?"

"That would be nice."

Jasmine watched Fredo disappear into the crowd, feeling warmth emanating throughout her body, but her smile dropped the moment her eyes locked with the light-skinned nigga. He mouthed the word bitch and started making his way over, eyes burning with rage.

Jasmine's grip on her Glock tightened, and she ran as fast as she could.

Viewer Discretion Advised

The music video set was booming by the time Caleb had arrived. His friend Rockit couldn't make it because he was laid up somewhere with his on and off again girlfriend.

Caleb ran out of pills the day before and his plug had been M.I.A. This situation occurred once in a blue moon, but the timing was terrible for Caleb. His depression was beating his ass and knowing that Bullet Tooth was out somewhere roaming the streets weighed on him heavily, and the pressure wasn't letting up.

He figured getting out the house would be good for him. Get some fresh air, and freeze the negativity out of his system. But he couldn't stop thinking about the conversation he had with the big-headed guy in the club.

Did he come for revenge? Was he revving up to do a drill in honor of Parks?

Caleb brought the gun with him and worried that he might use it if he ran into Park's killer. He wondered if the strange guy was telling the truth about Fredo and that this wasn't some elaborate set-up. Still, something about his words rang true and the message resonated with Caleb on levels that frightened him.

You're not a street nigga or a killer, Cal. You're an artist at your core. Your hands are built for pencils, paintbrushes, clay...what are you doing here?

Caleb took a puff on his joint, allowing the weed to calm his mind and loosen him up. His phone dinged and he checked his messages, opening a video from Rockit. He pressed play and watched as a muscular man pissed on Park's grave and laughed as he did it.

Something cracked inside Caleb, and anger rose like a vindictive apparition taking over his body. Venomous thoughts flooded his mind. He pressed a button on the side of his phone, shutting off the video as his head hurt, and it took everything in him not to throw the device. He took a deep pull on his joint, but it did nothing to dissipate the hot ball of anger mushrooming inside his gut. Through a cloud of smoke, he spotted the same man from the video in the crowd, and he tossed the joint aside.

Caleb's hand moved toward the inside of his coat, searching for the gun and keeping his eyes fixed on his target.

So that's him. That's the motherfucker who took Park's life.

The anger swelled up in his chest and the pain in Caleb's head intensified as he clutched the gun in his hand. He slowly made his way toward the man named Fredo.

Balaclava Sale

Fredo had no idea what he was doing at this video shoot, but running into Jasmine lifted his spirits. Gang members from different sets carried loaded guns in the open, smoking weed and drinking alcohol. The Vice Lords were outnumbered and he felt like this was a disaster waiting to happen.

Big Poliano preached about ending the violence between rival gangs, but his musical output promoted veiled threats, fucking bitches, popping pills, and sliding on the opps. He was busy rapping and throwing up gang signs in front of the camera. A violent energy emanated from the crowd, making Fredo uneasy. He was far from soft, but something about this shit wasn't right.

A man in a black balaclava aka the pooh shiesty, stood in the center of the crowd, smoking blunt after blunt after blunt. Something about this guy disturbed Fredo. He had a big head and kept whispering in people's ears.

Something was suspect about the nigga and Fredo wondered who invited this goofy to the video shoot and what gang he was affiliated with.

Fredo returned to the business at hand and tried striking up conversation with a few different people about guns, but no one gave a shit. He thought this would be the perfect place to get clientele, but people were stand-offish and borderline disrespectful.

These niggas are raising my blood pressure and this music ain't helping my cause.

Someone bumped into him and Fredo sighed, not understanding why people couldn't stay out of his way.

"Hold up, nigga. Who the fuck are you checking like that?"

The light-skinned nigga paused his pursuit and turned back towards Fredo.

"This doesn't concern you, fuck nigga."

"Oh yes it does, pussy boy."

The crowd watched as Fredo and the light-skinned nigga got in each other's faces, both toting guns. The entire set became eerily quiet and even Big Poliano stood there watching the confrontation unfold.

The directors kept filming, zooming in on the situation at hand. Potential b-roll for the video.

"You think I'm pussy?" The light skinned nigga asked, placing his big ass gun to the side of Fredo's head.

Fredo didn't flinch and felt no fear in his heart. This wasn't the first time someone had pulled a gun on him and probably wouldn't be the last.

"Smell like one and not the good kind either."

"Alright, bet." The light-skinned nigga pulled the trigger and his gun jammed. His eyes grew wide with confusion.

Fredo shoved his Glock in the man's chest and pulled the trigger with no hesitation, blowing a massive hole into his sternum. He went flying backward and blood spilled out in thick waves on the asphalt.

"That nigga wasn't fuckin around!" Someone in the crowd yelled.

"Should we call the cops?" One of the directors asked.

"No, someone move the body out the way, and let's keep it rolling," the other director commanded. "We spent too much money on this shit to stop now."

Armageddon Lane

Jasmine almost pissed herself when she heard the gunshots go off. She looked back and saw her pursuer bleeding out his back. Two men were moving him into someone's front yard like a bag of trash.

Her heart beat a million miles per minute, and she worried that she was on the brink of a heart attack. She had never seen some shit like this up close and personal. Despite having a challenging childhood and boatloads of trauma, she never saw anyone get shot. Every blue moon she heard gunshots in her neighborhood, but she never experienced death quite like this.

Calm down. Calm down. It's alright Jas. The guy's dead and you're safe. You're just panicking.

Jasmine didn't feel safe in her own skin, and she cursed herself for not speaking up and asking to stay by Fredo's side. She clutched her Glock and slowly walked back into the crowd, and squeezed the talisman in her pocket.

"You alright?" Fredo asked.

"Not really." Jasmine said.

"At least the nigga's dead."

"Yeah," Jasmine said.

A man wearing a balaclava laughed over and over, disturbing the peace and drawing attention to himself. Jasmine wondered if he was slow because no one else was joining in.

Big Poliano moved towards the man, growing more and more irritated. "Hey nigga, shut the fuck up. You're ruining the mood. Put the weed down."

"No, it's a free world and this display is hilarious."

"Naw nigga, this is my set and you're currently in my world. I will get you touched if you don't calm your funny looking ass down."

"I beg to differ." The man ripped off his balaclava, revealing an oversized head riddled with thick scar tissue and several bruises on his face. He grinned, showing off his mouth full of bullets.

"Oh shit, it's the nigga from the party we stomped out," someone in the crowd said. "Your face is fucked up."

Bullet Tooth raised two Polish Hellpup AK-47s with 100-round steel drums into the air and pulled the trigger, letting shots fly.

"Welcome to my world."

People screamed, and someone let off a flurry of shots, accidentally injuring other gang members. Chaos erupted on the set. The directors ran for cover, regretting the decision to film in the hood.

Big Poliano waved someone over and snatched a Glock 19X with a switch out of the man's hand, ready for action.

"Watch this pole talk, you dumb nigga."

The moment he pulled the trigger, his arm jerked to the left and the bullet ripped through a spectator's chest.

Bullet Tooth laughed as he unloaded one AK-47 into the crowd, bullets rocking bodies and blood splattering everywhere. "You don't possess the willpower to stop me Big Poliano, your gun is useless here. This is my domain."

One of Big Poliano's security guards threw a wild haymaker at Bullet Tooth, and he stepped out of the way. He tossed one of his guns aside and grabbed the guard by the shoulder, headbutting the man repeatedly until he crumpled to the ground, head indented and bleeding.

Bullet Tooth shoved the guard aside with the tip of his gun, enjoying the spectacle. He walked towards Big Poliano who struggled to aim his gun in Bullet Tooth's direction, caught underneath the psychic sway of the monstrosity, transfixed by his supremacy.

"Big Poliano—or should I call you Christopher—you should have left well enough alone and ran away. You're no hero, you're barely a gangster. That term used to carry weight, evoke a certain power, a camaraderie amongst men, a brotherhood. You smear the name... I mean, you use women as shields during shootouts, you pay others to do your bidding, you have nightmares of the members turning on you. Need I go on? The list is endless. You haven't really earned your stripes, now, have you?"

Big Poliano sniffled. "No..."

"Ah, finally some accountability. I respect that. Perhaps I should reward you."

Jasmine watched as Bullet Tooth grabbed the rapper's long chains and wrapped the excess length around his thick neck until his face began turning purple. Wheezing. Spittle flew out his mouth as the rapper choked, clutching at his neck, desperately gasping for air.

Big Poliano fell to his knees, barely conscious, and Bullet Tooth dragged him by a fistful of chains toward the cop cars, thick smoke spilling out into the night sky. He managed to lift up the sizeable rapper and tossed him into the purple flames.

"And that's the tragic end of Big Poliano. I'll send your mother my condolences and maybe I'll buy a shirt with your picture on it."

Bullet Tooth picked up one of his AK-47s and began hunting down the remaining survivors in the crowd. A few created makeshift blockades, letting off shots at the monstrosity and praying that one would be the charm.

Jasmine gasped when she saw Caleb push Fredo, catching him off guard. Caleb aimed a gun at Fredo's leg, pulling the trigger. Fredo's legs buckled, and he fell on his ass, clutching the wound.

"What the fuck are you doing?" Jasmine screamed.

"Stay out of this," Caleb said. "This nigga shot my friend and he has to pay."

"No, please stop!" Jasmine yelled.

Fredo struggled to get back to his feet. "I don't know you, nigga. We don't have beef."

Caleb moved closer, tears streaming down his face. "You killed my nigga Parks and then you pissed on his grave. That's beef, nigga."

Fredo opened his mouth to defend himself when he caught a stray bullet, ripping through his throat. He clawed at his adam's apple, struggling to breathe, blood sputtering out.

"Fuck!" Caleb yelled, pacing around in circles.

Jasmine bent down, cradling Fredo's head as blood dribbled out of his mouth and a red flower blossomed in his throat. She kissed his forehead after he took his last breath and grew still.

"You're responsible for this," Jasmine said, wiping her tears away. She got up and shoved Caleb.

"I-I wish I was," he staggered backward, struggling to regain his footing. "Nigga caught a stray."

"If you didn't shoot him in the leg—"

Five bodies were mowed down by a spray of bullets, each one falling directly in front of Jasmine and Caleb. They looked at each other and then back at Bullet Tooth who temporarily had his sights set on other people.

Oh fuck, fuck, fuck, fuck, fuck. Fuck me.

Jasmine was completely out of her element. She sprinted across the street, cursing her chunky soles, and her obsession with designer fashion. Ankles hurting from the exertion, she pushed through the pain, and climbed a wire fence, heaving herself over. Catching her breath, she watched the crowd continue to shoot one another.

"What the fuck is going on?"

She turned around and wrapped her arms around her knees, rocking back and forth. Her ears rang from the continuous barrage of gunshots. Might as well have been a warzone and she was hiding in the trenches. Pulling her phone out, she jabbed her PIN code in, but her signal was completely gone. She couldn't get through to anyone.

"Just my fucking luck."

A wet hand clamped over her mouth, dragging her into the grass. She tried screaming, but no one could hear her muffled cries over the gunshots.

She tried to aim her gun at the aggressor, fumbling to steady it, but she couldn't even get a good look at him to let off a shot. The hand disappeared and she was punched in the gut. The wind escaped her lungs, and she thought this might be the end.

The aggressor revealed himself as the balaclava-clad psychopath from earlier. Somehow, he had developed a gut and a considerable amount of weight everywhere else. Jasmine could have sworn that he was much skinnier five minutes ago. She wondered if her eyes were playing tricks on her or if something precious had broken deep inside her thanks to the trauma and violence she had endured.

"Jasmine, you weren't going to escape this shoot unscathed. Did you really think you were allowed to leave when the fun is only beginning?"

She kicked him in the nuts, and he hunched over, massaging his groin.

"What the fuck do you want from me?" She screamed, pulling her Glock up, and moving into her shooting stance. This is the moment she had trained tirelessly for.

Showtime.

"My pretty, dumb child," Bullet Tooth snickered. "You really think you can hurt me? You must be unfamiliar with my game. You are going to take that gun and kill yourself."

"No, I'm not, you sick bastard."

"Okay." A blue tongue unfurled from Bullet Tooth's mouth, dripping saliva. "Don't say I didn't warn you."

Jasmine turned the gun on herself, shoving the barrel underneath her chin. Her body wouldn't listen no matter how hard she willed her muscles to move. Tears ran down her cheeks as she realized what was about to take place.

"Please stop," she pleaded. "I'll do anything."

"No, child. Your first mistake was selling switches and getting involved in the lifestyle. The second was talking to that steroid concoction named Fredo. These two seemingly innocent events put you on a certain path inevitably leading to me."

"I don't give a fuck. Just let me go."

"My dear, you came here on your own accord. You drove here, parked, and walked to the video set. Did you not?"

"Yeah, but I didn't sign up to be in a shootout."

"That may be true, but here we are," Bullet Tooth licked his blubbery lips. "Join me in my crusade. Bring your fantasies to life. Take down the patriarchy with me."

"No, you cunt," Jasmine said. "You instigated this shit and if you didn't notice, you have a dick between your legs. You are the patriarchy."

Jasmine punched him in the face, clipping his jawline. Part of his skin smeared across her knuckles leaving a slimy residue. Blood dribbled down his bottom lip and he spit out a tooth—a bullet tooth. An 85gr T-REX copper bullet to be exact, designed to expand to nearly three times the original size, meant to take out large animals in the wild.

"Ouch, that hurt," Bullet Tooth said, massaging his dislocated jaw and snapping it back into place with a jarring *crack*. His skin billowed and puckered, features morphing into something softer, something more feminine. His rows of bullet teeth shrunk into his gumline and white teeth popped out. His eyes became kinder, warmer and his lips more sensual. His wavy features settled into the face of an older Palestinian woman, resembling the same woman Jasmine called mom in the depths of her dreams. A white hijab wrapped itself around her head, covering her hair and neck, flowing down to her chest.

"M-Mom," Jasmine said, feeling like her world was being ripped apart. "Is that you?"

"Yes dear, I've been waiting for you for so long. I didn't think I would have survived the bombs, the starvation, the lack of electricity and clean water without the thought of seeing my own flesh and blood again. As Allah is my witness, I sacrificed everything to come back to you."

"They told me you died..."

"I love you, Jasmine." Her mother's wrinkled face pouted, smile lines drooping downwards. "Don't you recognize your own mother?"

Jasmine's heart swelled—on the verge of shattering into a thousand pieces. The safety she felt emanating off the woman in front of her was undeniable. Her mother's warmth broke through the igloo she forged around her own heart for the last 16 years. Finally melting. She could let her guard down for once and breathe.

"I'm sorry, it's just been so long... can I touch you?" Jasmine said, desperately needing to confirm that this was real and not some fever dream she concocted.

"Yes, my dear. I've been waiting for us to rekindle our relationship, waiting for your embrace. This is what mother and daughters look like."

Jasmine smiled weakly, stepping forward, fingers outstretched. She touched her mother's face, feeling soft skin, tracing a couple of wrinkles. Kindness and maternal love dripped off her mother. Her cheeks rippled, liver spots expanding, tremors moving underneath her features like a wave.

"Are you okay, mom?" Jasmine said, confused.

"I'm not okay. I haven't been okay since you left me in that open-air prison."

"I-I didn't know. They told me you were killed...that you died."

"A part of me died, the day your dad was crushed underneath rubble from a bomb. Soldiers cleaved the skin from his corpse and harvested his organs for science, for the greater good."

Jasmine sobbed, imagining her dad's corpse being treated like an afterthought. Something to be dug into, another brown body to be excavated and colonized, stripping her father of any value even in the afterlife.

"Everyone said I was so lucky to have survived, but for what? To live the rest of my days alone. I wept in darkness for 100 days and 100 nights."

Her mom opened her trench coat revealing dappled flesh, crisscrossed with stitches, gaping wounds that barked secrets in their ugliness, and the tell-tale signs of bullet wounds—purplish scars weaving tragic tales of her homeland. Her breasts were barely contained by her large purple bra, flesh spilling out the sides, pulled down to the earth by gravity.

"Look at me!"

Jasmine let the waterfall of tears cascade down her face, not caring how she looked any longer.

"Women give birth, but we know death all too well," her mother continued with clenched fists. "We straddle that space between worlds, we carry the burdens of boys who call themselves men, we nurture those who can't nurture themselves even if the divine womb is destroyed."

Jasmine buried her hands in her face, not being able to face the woman she called her mother, not being able to digest the bitter truths washing over her.

"Stop with the theatrics, child," her mother scoffed. "Where the fuck were you?"

"I-I was..."

"Too busy showing off your body on the internet and waving guns. Preaching about feminism, talking about a country you haven't returned back to since you were three. You make a mockery of Allah and you bring dishonor to your family. You should be ashamed of yourself!"

Jasmine's sobs hitched in her chest, panic sinking in like a blade of ice. *How could I be so foolish*, she thought. *I'm a horrible daughter*. She stumbled forward, searching for comfort from what she thought was her mother, arms wrapped around the woman in front of her, hanging on for dear life as if this woman could erase her shame, erase her guilt, and make the world right again.

Through blurred sight and tear droplets stuck to her eyelashes, Jasmine saw something both extraordinary and terrifying unfolding in her mother's visage.

The soft features rippled, and the nose cracked, cartilage jutting forward, stretching into a snout. A shock of brown fur erupted from her cheeks and spread across her face. Every feminine feature was sucked into oblivion. Two skinny horns ripped out of her black hair, curling backward in a stygian loop.

The Nubian Ibex, a desert-dwelling goat, which populated Jasmine's homeland stared back at her. Only this Ibex was the size of a grown man, mucus dripping down its cold nose. It bleated, a bass-heavy sound, more like an aggressive shriek.

Jasmine recoiled, stepping back slowly. There were about five thousand Nubian Ibex left in the wild. Classified as vulnerable, but at this moment she felt a strange kinship with the animal. Standing on the brink of extinction, she felt like she had nothing to lose, that she already had been forced to climb the edge of a steep rock face and somehow she still found her footing in the most precarious crags.

"Why are you looking at me like that, my dear?" The goat said, snorting, voice still soft and wizened. "I thought you loved me."

"I don't love you. You're dead," Jasmine wiped her eyes with the back of her hand, slick with tears. She reached for her gun. "This is some sick mirage. Stop fucking with my head!"

Jasmine raised her Glock back up, taking advantage of the bodily autonomy she had. She aimed at the center of mass, took a breath and pulled the trigger, but nothing happened. The bullet felt like it was lodged in the gun. Pulling the trigger repeatedly, Jasmine fumed at the inaction of the weapon.

"My child you can't shoot your own mother," the goatman waved his index finger back and forth. "That's haram."

Bullet Tooth's face undulated, hairy flesh swelling and returning back to normal. He ripped the hijab into shreds, took a deep inhale, and his dark red eyes dilated with ecstasy. "Ah that was fun. You stay right there while I indulge myself on this pain and agony in the air. What a time to be alive!"

Jasmine couldn't move and she found the gun aimed back herself, jammed against the underbelly of her chin. The sound of cracking and popping filled her ears. It reminded her of her short-lived trips to the chiropractor a few years back. An attempt at fixing her posture, but that sudden crack, the gas and pressure being released in her joints did nothing to dissuade the existential terror she felt inside those large palms, knowing that her body could be so easily manipulated by forces beyond her control. These were the sounds of Bullet Tooth's nauseating growth, each limb growing bigger, his stomach rising like yeast, skin swelling to absurd proportions. He was forced to take a seat on the asphalt and his psychic vice grip loosened momentarily as Jasmine removed the gun from her chin.

"This is such a lovely feast I'm having," he licked his finger, sucking on an invisible sustenance only he could witness. "I love Chicago. It has such a bad reputation, but I have no idea why. I should visit more often."

Jasmine's custom Glock fell to the ground and melted into a black polymer and metal sludge. Fizzling in the winter night. Jasmine cried, feeling trapped in this hellish predicament with this foul *thing* that had the audacity to masquerade as her mother. Then she remembered the talisman, desperately hoping it would ward off the monstrosity from doing anything else fucked up.

She pulled out the talisman and waved it in the air like a cross.

Bullet Tooth laughed. "Your silly trinket can't stop me, child. Just as pointless as holy water or sage. Plus, that's meant for protection, not offensive measures of any kind."

Jasmine threw it at Bullet Tooth, calling his bluff. He winced in response, picking up the talisman and snapping it in half, tossing it down his gullet.

"No more protection for the Palestinian princess. How sad."

Jasmine felt hopeless and defeated. The tears came back full force.

"Wipe your tears, child. The night is still young and there's fun to be had."

Alleyway Vendetta

Everything inside Caleb told him to go home and leave well enough alone, but he couldn't do that. Adrenaline flowed through his veins, and he was on edge as he carefully stepped over two bodies, one being Fredo. He searched for Bullet Tooth, feeling that same electric energy he felt the night he summoned the monstrosity, thrumming through the air like loose wires.

Sirens rang in the distance. A dog barked repeatedly, and gunshots still peppered the air like a warzone. Caleb knew Bullet Tooth orchestrated all of this, and he had to put an end to this shit once and for all.

Caleb searched the block for some sign of the bastard as he moved into an alley. He looked up at the full moon, luminous and sickly bright in the night sky.

A black cat ran down the alley, taking cover in someone's backyard. Caleb followed the trail, headed in the direction the cat originally came from. He spotted the girl who blamed him for Fredo's death looking absolutely horrified at something rustling in the darkness.

Moving in closer, Caleb saw Bullet Tooth on his back, in the middle of a dramatic transformation, blue tongue hanging out, mouth frothing.

"My child, you found me. Please join us. We can be one big happy family."

"You're related?" Jasmine cringed.

"Hell no, we're not related. He just loves calling everyone a child. Disrespectful as hell."

"I was about to say," Jasmine said, crossing her arms. "What are you doing here?"

"I have to end him."

"End me?" Bullet Tooth asked. "The occultists couldn't stop me, the Vikings couldn't stop me, the Egyptians couldn't stop me, your poor excuse for a government couldn't stop me...what makes you think this outcome will be any different?"

Bullet Tooth gorged himself on the violent energy pulsing in the atmosphere, skin ballooning outward at a rapid pace, stretching like dough instead of flesh. His once skinny body grew seven times larger, thick rolls of fat running up and down his absurd frame. His clothes were in complete tatters, hanging off his inflated limbs. He was nearly naked, lying on his back. His monstrous dick throbbing and hard, bounced on the pavement, precum dripping out the tip.

"This is glorious. I thought the Dark Ages were full of savages, but this is something special."

Jasmine vomited at the sight of Bullet Tooth's gluttonous transformation and his nasty member hanging down his enormous thigh. She wiped her mouth with her sleeve.

"That shit is disgusting."

Caleb looked down at the gun in his hand and raised it upward. He wondered if he had the guts to do what he knew he needed to. He had never killed a man before, let alone an otherworldly entity with a penchant for violence.

"C'mon, what are you waiting for?" Jasmine said, zipping up her jacket. The temperature felt like it had dropped considerably since the shooting began. "You were ready to murder Fredo earlier. What happened to that energy?"

"That was different...He killed my friend Parks."

"Look I get that was personal, but this motherfucker is going to kill everybody we love if you don't end this," Jasmine said, trying to speak some sense into Caleb. "And he's not even human. Look at it."

Bullet Tooth's bloodshot eyes rolled into the back of his head, laughing at their conversation. His gaunt face dropped downward as if it was constructed of raw dough. He continued growing in size, resembling a blimp in the alley.

"Honor me, Caleb. Listen to my words very carefully. They're of the utmost importance. Murder that bitch." Bullet Tooth demanded.

Jasmine backed up, clutching her zipper. She never felt so vulnerable, especially without a gun in hand. Frightened at the possibility of Caleb turning on her, thick tears ran down her face.

"I-I know we don't know each other like that, but please don't shoot me," Jasmine pleaded. "He's just trying to fuck with your head. Don't listen to him. Push that bastard out. You're stronger than this."

Caleb knew she was right. The bastard's words were like parasites crawling around his mind, pushing him, urging him to listen to the reptilian part of his brain.

"Don't worry, I'm not going to kill you. I got it under control."

Bullet Tooth snickered with glee. "Caleb, don't listen to that *female*. This cold world has hurt you, cut you deep. Killed your best friend, filled you with sadness and depression. This is your chance for retribution. Grab hold of this opportunity. Rise up and be a man. Manifest destiny here and now."

Caleb's grip on his gun tightened and he felt his hand rising, turning the barrel in Jasmine's direction.

"What the fuck are you doing?" Jasmine yelled. "I thought you said you weren't going to kill me. You just said you had it under control."

Feeling horrible and guilty, Caleb focused his willpower on lifting his finger off the trigger, but it was as if his body was moving on its own accord and Bullet Tooth was manipulating every move.

Bullet Tooth smirked. "There's nothing you can do you filthy cunt. Today is a day of reckoning. You might as well embrace death."

Caleb put both hands on the gun, steadying the aim. He didn't want to kill Jasmine, but he felt like the outcome was inevitable. His eyes grew wet as he briefly considered killing himself.

"Do it, my child," Bullet Tooth commanded. "Take out your anger on this woman. Unleash your frustrations. You know you want to. I could feel it inside you when you confronted Fredo. Discard your moral compass and feel the ultimate freedom, the liberation that comes with murder."

"No," Caleb said defiantly. "I won't."

"It will transform you. Empower you. Enlighten you. You humans fear murder when you should just give into your animal instincts. That's what you truly are at the end of the day. Animals."

"Bulla, I'm not going kill anyone especially not for you."

Bullet Tooth paused, looking stunned. "How dare you call me by my true name. Where did you learn that, scum?"

Caleb's index finger began to loosen, hands less tight, slowly gaining power back over his own body and his gun. Without thinking, he turned the gun on Bullet Tooth and shot him in the gut repeatedly until the gun was spent.

Bullet Tooth's blimp-like body exploded. Bones, limbs, and bullets went flying in all directions. Caleb covered Jasmine's body with his own, feeling debris bounce off his back.

"Are you okay?" Caleb asked. "I'm so sorry. I almost killed you."

"Yeah, thanks for saving me, but you're a piece of shit for killing my friend."

She backhanded Caleb. "That's for Fredo."

"I probably deserve that." Caleb rubbed his cheek, gun hanging by his side. "My name's Caleb by the way."

"I'm Jasmine. I hope there's no hard feelings. Just had to get that out of my system."

"I get it."

"I'll have to repay you one of these days. You did save me."

"No rush. I'm still coming down from everything."

Flaps of skin, pieces of bones, and a pile of bullets were all that remained of Bullet Tooth. The spot previously occupied by the monstrosity was smoking and wet.

"Do you think it's dead?" Jasmine asked. "Like for real?"

"I don't think it was ever truly alive. But that nigga's gone."

"How do you know?"

"Trust me, I know."

The Art of Winning

Caleb walked on stage in front of an auditorium jam-packed with students and faculty. The crowd clapped as he accepted a gold trophy for first place in the art show. His art pieces were prominently displayed on stands behind him and a mysterious art collector named "O" had purchased every single one. The money would be benefitting the school and part of it going towards improving the art program.

He couldn't believe he actually won the competition, and his first two years of college tuition would be paid for. For years he dreamed of attending the Savannah College of Art and Design, and it looked like this long-standing dream would finally come to fruition.

Caleb's classmates clapped and Miss Kerrigan nudged him towards the mic hanging from the wooden podium. Caleb walked up and adjusted the mic to his height.

"I just want to say thank you. I never knew my art could be my way out the city and the door to a new life. It's been a hard year for many of us, but nigga we made it."

The crowd erupted into a frenzy of applause, yelling, and whistles. As Caleb raised his trophy to the sky, he smiled for the first time in ages, relishing the joy and sense of accomplishment running through his body.

Jasmine carefully placed her phone inside a mini-tripod holder. Satisfied with the positioning, she fixed her hair and pressed the go live emblem as she buzzed with anticipation.

"Hey babes, I'm back. I'm sorry it's been so long since I've gone live, but I've been going through some personal issues and needed a mental health break from social media. I'm in a much better space though. I was going to do a gun tour since everyone was so patient, but I have something special I want to share with you."

She fake screamed with joy as she pulled out a box wrapped in black paper.

"This is prolly what you think it is. Today's the big day we've all been waiting for."

Jasmine ripped the wrapping paper apart and pulled open the box, unveiling a gun case. She undid the clasps and rubbed her hands together. Proudly displaying the Draco AK-47 in her small hands, she turned it around in a full circle for the phone's camera. Hearts flooded the screen and fans donated a heap of digital roses.

"Damnnnnnnnnnnn, those niggas in Romania really know how to make a gun."

Jasmine posed with the gun from multiple angles and stuck her tongue out.

"I'm taking this baby to the gun range tomorrow. Alright, it was fun, babes. And like I always say... hennything's possible."

She blew the camera a kiss and ended the live.

Dumpster Diving Lovebirds

A cluster of rats scurried over bags of frozen trash piled in a green dumpster. A white woman named Susan bent over the lip of the dumpster, digging around, searching for gold. Susan pulled her thick scarf down to speak to her boyfriend.

"Hunter, come over here. I found something special."

Hunter ran over with a black trash bag in hand. "What did you find? Anything good?"

"A couple Gucci boxes and some V-H-S tapes."

"Wow, when's the last time we've had a movie night?"

"It's been ages, love. You ready for a trip down memory lane?"

"I think so. I'm just worried this might be some weird movie or homemade porn. I don't want to watch something obscene."

"Says 'Project Bullet Baby' on this sticker. Can't be that bad right?"

"I'm probably overreacting. Let's give it a shot."

"That's the spirit. We'll make some popcorn, drink some Moscow mules, and watch it Thursday night. It'll be a nice date."

"You only live once, right?" Hunter poked his lips out and Susan kissed him passionately.

"I love you."

"I love you more."

The VHS tapes softly whirred inside the trash bag and Bullet Tooth stirred in his sleep, not quite ready to be reawakened.

Acknowledgements

This book has been a long time coming. I first pitched this to J. David Osborne in 2014 along with *Black Gypsies* for Broken River Books. He chose *Black Gypsies* for good reason. I was too naive. My writing katana needed to be sharpened and my creative arsenal needed time to mature. Well, I guess we made it, right? Special thanks to JDO, Kelby Losack, David Simmons, and E. Rathke. They provided constant support, encouragement, and suggestions. Shoutout to Chief Keef, FBG Duck, no auto tune Lil Durk, Billionaire Black, Muslimgauze, Danny Brown, Lil Peep, and Lil Tracy for spiritual inspiration. Shoutout to Daniel Vlasaty, Ryan Jackson, Lucas Mangum, and Cece as well. Nigga, we made it.

About the Author

GRANT WAMACK is the author of *God's Leftovers*, *Black Gypsies*, and *The Hum of the World & Other Stories*. He has more than forty short stories published in places such as *Dark Moon Digest*, *The Best of Surreal Grotesque*, and *The New Flesh*. When he's not writing, he's reading tarot cards, practicing jiu jitsu, and smoking weed in LA. You can follow his come-up over at his newsletter Literary Loud:

  https://grantwamack.substack.com/